THE HEIR FROM NOWHERE

BY

TRISH MOREY

MILLS & BOON

All the characters in this book have no existence outside the imagination of the author, and have no relation whatsoever to anyone bearing the same name or names. They are not even distantly inspired by any individual known or unknown to the author, and all the incidents are pure invention.

First published in Great Britain 2011
Harlequin Mills & Boon Limited,
Eton House, 18-24 Paradise Road, Richmond, Surrey TW9 1SR

© Trish Morey 2011

ISBN: 978 0 263 88642 9

Harlequin Mills & Boon policy is to use papers that are natural, renewable and recyclable products and made from wood grown in sustainable forests. The logging and manufacturing process conform to the legal environmental regulations of the country of origin.

Printed and bound in Spain
by Litografia Rosés, S.A., Barcelona

THE HEIR FROM NOWHERE

CHAPTER ONE

'You don't know me, but I'm having your baby.'

Was it possible for your blood to stop flowing before you were dead? Dominic Pirelli believed it, the way his veins suddenly clamped shut and his blood seemed to congeal in a heart that had itself long ago turned to stone. And even if he'd wanted to slam the phone down in denial, he was incapable of movement, one hundred per cent of his energy concentrated and distilled down, focused on just one tiny word.

No!

And then the need to breathe kicked in and he dragged in air, and slowly his pulse resumed, pounding out a message in his temples, echoing his disbelief. It was impossible! It didn't matter what the doctor had tried to tell him this morning. It didn't matter what this woman was telling him now. It had to be impossible.

'...having your baby.'

The words played over and over in his brain, defying logic, making no sense. He dragged in air, trying to re-establish a foothold in a day gone mad.

This was not the way he was used to operating. On a normal day it took a lot to blindside Dominic Pirelli. Many a business competitor had tried to gain an advantage over him and been unsuccessful, washed away in the wake he left behind as he forged ahead with his own plans. Many a woman had tried to tie the billion-aire investor down and failed, swept aside like so many brightly coloured petals on a fast-flowing stream.

On a normal day, nothing happened in his life that he didn't professionally desire or personally sanction.

But today had ceased being a normal day one short, cataclysmic hour ago.

When the clinic had called with the news.

A mistake, he'd first assumed.

An impossibility.

It was so many years ago and someone had clearly pulled the wrong name from its files; someone had clear-ly rung the wrong number. And he'd argued exactly that, only to be told that the only mistake had occurred some three months back, when the wrong embryo had some-how been put in the wrong woman. And even through the torrent of apologies, he'd still refused to believe it could be true.

And then the phone had rung a second time and a woman's voice uttered the words that turned a horrific concept into chilling reality.

'I'm having your baby.'

He sank heavily into his chair, wheeling it around so that he could see something—anything—other than the nightmare that consumed his thoughts and vision. But the view he knew should be there, the picture-perfect view over a glittering Sydney Harbour, the yachts and ferries zipping their way beneath the Harbour Bridge and between the park-lined shores, was lost to him in a blur of incredulity. He squeezed his eyes shut and pinched his nose so hard that fireworks shot through his closed lids, but still nowhere near hard enough to blot out the anguish or the pain.

This could not be happening!

Not this way.

It was never supposed to happen this way!

'Mr Pirelli…' The voice resumed. Hesitant. Shaky. Almost as if the caller were as shocked as he was. *Not a chance.* 'Are you still there?'

He exhaled. Long and loud, not caring how it sounded down the line. He didn't care about anything right now, least of all about sounding civil. 'Why are you doing this?' he heard himself say. 'What's in it for you?'

He heard a gasp, a muffled cry and almost felt sorry for speaking his mind. Almost. But he'd only spoken the truth. Experience told him that people rarely did anything if not motivated by profit.

'I just thought, given the circumstances, you should be informed.'

'Like hell.'

A pause. 'I'm sorry. I can't help how you see it. I just wanted to talk to you. To see if we can find some way through this mess.'

This mess. At least she had that right. 'You think there's some way through this? You think there's some simple solution that can be plucked from the air? Do you have fairies in the bottom of your garden, or simply in your head?'

He expected she'd hang up. He'd hoped she would, if only to terminate a conversation he didn't want to have—wasn't equipped to have.

Because he wasn't sure he could hang up first. He was no more equipped to close off the chance of—what exactly?—the chance of having a child that had long since died, along with his marriage?

But there was no telling click at the end of the line to momentarily assuage his pain and relieve what little guilt he felt. No sound but a pause that grew heavier and weightier by the second. Until he found himself inexplicably awaiting her response. What was she thinking? What did she really want? Fifteen plus years building the biggest business empire Australia had seen had left him woefully unprepared for anything like this.

'I know this has been a shock,' she said softly. 'I understand.'

'Do you? I doubt it.'

'This is hard for me too!' Her voice sounded more strident, more pained. 'Do you really think I was overjoyed to discover that I was pregnant with your child?'

His child? The realisation slammed into him like a blow to the gut. No mere concept; this woman was carrying *his* child. His and Carla's. The child she'd been so desperate to have. The child she'd been unable to conceive. Even success through their last resort, IVF, had eluded her, cycle after futile cycle. He put a hand to his brow, felt the shock of events thunder in the beat of blood at his temples, tasted the bitter taste of bile in the back of his throat.

And yet this woman—this stranger—had succeeded where Carla had failed so very many times.

Why?

Who was this woman that she could turn his life upside down? Who was she that she could stir up the ghosts of his past? Who gave her the right to mess with his life?

All he knew was that he couldn't do this over the phone. He had to meet her. Had to deal with this face to face.

He tugged on his tie, undid his top button, but still the room felt sticky and overheated. And still his voice, when it came, felt like gravel in his throat. It sounded worse. 'What did you say your name was again?'

'It's Angie. Angie Cameron.'

'Look, Miss Cameron—'

'It's Mrs, actually, but just Angie is fine.'

Of course. He pushed back in his chair. She might sound like some nervous teenager over the phone, but she would have to be married and for some years to be undergoing fertility treatment. 'Look, Mrs Cameron,' he said, ignoring her invitation for informality when he was still having trouble believing her story, 'this isn't something I can discuss over the phone.'

'I understand.'

He sucked air into his lungs and shook his head. God, did she have to sound like some kind of therapist? If she was so upset about carrying his child, then why didn't she rant and scream and rail about injustice in the world like he wanted to? Didn't she realise his world was tearing apart—the world he'd taken years to rebuild?

He could so not do this!

'We should meet,' he said somehow through near-gritted teeth as he wheeled around in his chair, his finger resting over a button on the phone that would connect him to Simone. 'As soon as possible. I'll put you back to my PA. She'll organise the details.'

If she had anything else to say, he didn't hear it before he punched that button and slammed the receiver down, lungs burning as if he'd just run ten kilometres along the cliffs, his brow studded with sweat. Simone could deal with it. Simone was good with tidying up after him while he worked out what came next.

And what did come next? What followed the disbelief?

Anger, he recognised, as the blood pounded loud in

his ears and fire burned hot in his gut. Right now anger boiled up inside him like lava looking for an exit—lava ready to burst him apart like a volcano set to erupt.

Because the impossible had happened.

The unthinkable.

And somebody was going to pay!

CHAPTER TWO

ANGIE set the receiver down, her hand still trembling, her cheeks damp with tears. But what had she expected? That the man would welcome the news she was carrying his child as if it was some kind of miracle?

Hardly. She swiped at her cheeks with the back of her hand, pulled a tissue from a box and blew her nose. After all, it hadn't felt like any kind of miracle when she'd been given the news. Far from it.

Still, did he have to sound so angry? Anyone would think it was all her fault.

She put a guilty hand over her still flat stomach, home to the child she'd never really wanted, the child she'd only agreed to have because Shayne had so desperately wanted a son, the child that had turned out not to be his.

Maybe it was her fault.

Unnatural, Shayne had called her. A real woman would want babies, he'd said, saving the most hurtful for when they had to cancel a holiday in order to scrape together the money for the procedures because he'd managed to get a subsidised place in the Carmichael Clinic, the best fertility clinic in Australia.

A real woman wouldn't need IVF to get pregnant.

And then, when finally the IVF had succeeded and

she was pregnant and it looked like Shayne would have the child he'd wanted so desperately, the clinic had called with the news of their terrible mix-up and she was a failure once again.

Because a real woman wouldn't want to carry another man's baby. Because a real woman would take the clinic up on their generous offer to fix it.

Maybe Shayne was right.

Maybe this was her punishment for not being a real woman. Cursed with a child she'd never really wanted and that wasn't even hers, and yet unable to bring herself, as Shayne had so eloquently put it, to fix it.

Fix it.

He'd made it sound so simple, like taking out the rubbish or tossing away old clothes. But this wasn't about a bag of trash. She wasn't carrying around a bag of old clothes. Whether or not she'd wanted it, there was a baby growing inside her belly. A life. Someone else's child.

And after all the effort the clinic had gone to, all the tests and injections and procedures and hand-holding to get her pregnant, they thought they could just turn around and somehow make it better?

It was never going to happen.

Besides, it wasn't only her decision to make. Not when there was a couple out there who'd put their heart and soul into creating this new life. Not when this child was rightfully theirs. Whatever happened now, whatever they decided, *at the very least* they deserved to know of this baby's existence.

She squeezed her eyes shut as her fingers curled into the denim of her shorts. Poor baby, to end up with her of all people, the woman who never really wanted a child in the first place, the woman who'd only agreed in order to save her marriage.

What a joke!

'I'm sorry, baby. But we'll meet your dad soon. Maybe even your mum too. They'll want you, I'm sure.'

And if they didn't?

A solitary tear slid down her cheek as she thought back to the phone call, remembering the deep and damning tones of the man's voice, as if she'd been to blame for visiting upon him some momentous disaster. Then again, it probably felt like some momentous disaster to him right now. She'd gone through the same stages herself. The shock. The disbelief. The sheer bewilderment that came with discovering that a mistake so fundamental could have occurred in a medical facility, a place that was supposed to specialize in making dreams come true, not in creating nightmares.

And then she'd borne the full brunt of Shayne's reactions. He'd gone from shock to fury in the space of a heartbeat. Fury that the baby he'd been bragging about to family and friends for a month wasn't his at all. Fury with the clinic for messing with his plans. Fury that had changed direction and headed straight for her when she'd refused point-blank to have the abortion the clinic had offered and that he'd demanded.

Oh, yes, she understood full well how shell-shocked Mr Pirelli would be feeling right now. But for all his aggravation, for all his strident accusation, he could have hung up on her. He could have simply denied the child was his.

But he had taken her call and he had agreed to meet her tomorrow. And right now that was the best she could bequeath to the tiny baby growing deep inside her—the chance for it to be with its real parents, the people who had gone through hell and back to create it, the people who had first rights to this child.

A car slowed outside. She glanced up at the clock on the wall above her head, saw that it was almost six and for just a moment imagined it must be Shayne home from the foundry, and for just a moment panicked that she hadn't started dinner yet.

Before a pain still jagged and raw ripped through her as she remembered.

Shayne wasn't coming home any more.

She was alone.

The Darling Harbour boardwalk was crowded and congested with holidaymakers taking videos and eating ice creams, vying for space with performers busking for spare change. Seagulls squawked both overhead and underfoot, fighting each other for crumbs, while a reproduction sailing ship spewed a hundred excited tourists back onto the wharf.

Dominic sighed, feeling out of place as he and Simone waited near the designated meeting spot and half wishing his PA had chosen somewhere less public and more private for this meeting, but then the crowds were apparently half the attraction. Keep it informal, Simone had suggested. On neutral territory. Away from his lawyer's offices, which might give the impression he was ready to broker some kind of deal. Away from the Pirelli building where his wealth was obvious as soon as you stepped into the stunning marble lobby. This Mrs Cameron might have pretended to be making some kind of altruistic gesture, but he had no proof of that. There was no point putting temptation right in front of her.

Simone had a point, he'd conceded, catching a whiff of her expensive perfume amidst the salt and popcorn-tinged air. It was her favourite, he recognised, the one he'd given her a bottle of last Christmas. It suited her.

Sleek and no-nonsense, feminine without being flowery. Exactly, in fact, like she was and exactly what he needed in a PA.

Come to think of it, Simone had been right about this place, he revised, peeling off his jacket and hooking it over his shoulder. He could be anonymous here, no longer Dominic Pirelli, billionaire investor and market strategist, but just one more suit escaping his office for an hour.

Except that this suit was waiting to meet the woman who was carrying his child.

Anticipation coiled in his gut. He glanced down at the platinum Tag Heuer at his wrist, saw that she was already late.

'Do you think she'll turn up?' Simone looked over her shoulder, putting voice to his greatest fear, her asymmetrical black bob swinging around her head. 'What if she changes her mind? She didn't leave a contact number.'

'She'll turn up,' he said, willing the woman to show. After the way he'd spoken to her yesterday, he'd be the last to be surprised she was having second thoughts, but it didn't matter if she had changed her mind. He had her name. She had his baby. And there was no way she was escaping him now. 'She'll turn up.'

Angie's eyes felt heavy and scratchy as she hurried along the pedestrian bridge linking the hurly-burly of Sydney CBD streets to the tourist precinct of Darling Harbour, and she didn't need to see her reflection to know how red they appeared to the outside world. She could tell that from the inside.

Screams had driven her from sleep and dreams filled with snarling dogs snapping and tugging at her clothes and body. One had taken Shayne's face while it circled barking out his taunts, telling her she would never be a real woman. Another had soothed her with words of comfort while trying to snatch her baby at the same time. And yet another had taken his place, larger and more powerful than all the rest, growling with teeth bared, moving closer, ready to savage.

And she'd woken in fear to her own screams, panting and desperate, the sheets knotted around her, her body damp with perspiration and her lonely bed more empty than ever. But safe, she'd realised, blessedly safe from the nightmare.

After that it had been impossible to sleep, the images the night had spun leaving her shaken and afraid, the night sounds of Sherwill—the barking dogs, the squeal of tyres as the hoons did burn-outs around the streets, the neighbours yelling—all keeping her company while a hundred scenarios for how today's meeting would unfold spun their way through her mind. No wonder she hadn't slept.

And now the light summer breeze whipped at her hair, carrying with it a combination of diesel fumes from the highway below and greasy doughnuts from a nearby stall and Angie's stomach roiled anew. She protested at the unfairness. There was nothing left in her stomach, and yet still she wanted to heave.

Please God, she thought, swallowing back on the urge. Not now. Not here. Not when she was rushing to get to this meeting. She'd lost breakfast—one piece of dry toast and a cup of tea—ten minutes after she'd pointlessly forced it down, and that had been hours ago. An hour on a jostling, crowded train hadn't helped, nor had the man who had lurched against her from behind as she'd left the train and almost sent her sprawling to the platform. He'd disappeared into the crowds without a word of apology, while she'd had to sit down for ten minutes to see out the cold sweat and wait for her heartbeat and temperature to get back under control.

Ten minutes she hadn't had.

So much for being relaxed and composed before she met the father of the child growing inside her.

Damn.

She blinked against the lunch-time sun, pushing her sunglasses higher on her nose as she descended the last few steps to the crowded boardwalk, suddenly wishing she'd worn something lighter. She'd wanted to cover herself up but it was much too hot for jeans and her old cardigan and she felt tatty and dated. Families strolled by as she hesitated on the last step, speaking in languages she didn't recognise, the children laughing with painted faces and hanging on to fat balloons that bounced against the air as they ran. Couples walked hand in hand, sharing secrets, oblivious to everything and everyone. Lunch-time joggers darted between them all, all lean limbed and firm skinned under Lycra and nylon and wired for sound.

Angie pulled her thin discount department store cardigan tighter around her shoulders as she made her way through the crowds, half wishing she'd never agreed to a meeting here. Darling Harbour had sounded both cosmopolitan and exotic when she'd heard Mr Pirelli's secretary suggest it as the meeting location and she'd made out she knew exactly where she was supposed to be, too embarrassed to admit she hadn't been here for years.

Besides, she'd been so relieved that he'd agreed to meet her at all, she wasn't about to argue about the location.

It was a good sign, wasn't it, that he wanted to meet

her? And if he met with her, surely that meant he would want the child? She held that hope close to her heart, nurtured it. It was all she wanted, for this child to be with its rightful parents, to be cherished by them.

And if they decided they didn't want it?

She sucked in a mouthful of the salt-tinged air. Well, there were other options, other couples unable to have children who would adore a tiny baby as their own. This baby would make someone happy, she was sure of it.

She pulled a crumpled note from her pocket, checked again for the details of where she was supposed to meet and scanned the surroundings, feeling a sizzle of apprehension when she recognised the green arch of the Harbourside Shopping Centre the PA had told her to wait outside. Her steps slowed as she approached. She was close now but, with the shifting crowd milling around the water's edge, it was impossible to pick out individuals. What if he hadn't waited? What if he'd given up and left?

Then, as she drew closer, she saw a couple sitting at a table holding hands, their heads bowed, the mood intense. She hesitated, her heart thudding hard in her chest. Could they be them? Could this be the parents of the child growing inside her?

Even as she watched, she saw the woman swipe tears from the corners of her eyes. Angie felt those tears like a tug against her womb. Surely it must be them? This was the right place and she was late. Was that why she was crying—because she feared Angie wasn't going to show?

Yet still she wavered, unwilling to intrude on this private moment. She looked around, shifting from one foot to the other, searching for any other more likely looking couple. There was a party of Japanese students lining the edge of the boardwalk, and an Italian family seated at a nearby table enjoying gelati and then there was a man in a white shirt with his jacket slung over his shoulder standing with his back to her.

Her eyes almost skated over him.

Almost.

All too soon they skated back. He stood tall and dark and somehow compelling, even from this angle, and when he turned his head to talk to the slim woman Angie had missed standing beside him, his profile only added to his appeal. A strong nose and jaw, and a dark slash of brows atop eyes that seemed focused on the woman beside him.

Another couple, she surmised, and way too unlikely. The woman looked cool and collected and nowhere near anxious enough to be meeting the woman inadvertently carrying her child, while surely he was too perfect, too virile-looking. For even while she knew fertility had nothing to do with looks, somehow the prospect that this man needed help seemed too far-fetched. Her eyes slipped away. And then she heard a cry of anguish and turned in time to see the woman on the bench jump up, the man reaching for her hand to stop her.

Guilt consumed her. She shouldn't have been so late. She should never have hesitated and added to her distress. She dragged in air, desperate to find a way through the sudden tangle her nerves had become, forcing herself to take the few tentative steps towards the couple.

'Over there. Could that be them?'

Dominic's eyes followed in the direction Simone indicated, settling on a couple sitting at a table not far away. He sucked in air. Could this be the woman who'd called? Was the man sitting alongside her husband? They were clearly not tourists, not the way they were dressed, and the woman's expression, her tightly drawn features and reddened eyes signalled that something was definitely not right between them.

Could it be because she was carrying someone else's child? Carrying his?

Breath whooshed from his lungs as every organ inside him contracted. Was the child Carla had so desperately and futilely wanted somehow growing inside this woman instead?

He studied the couple while he willed his breathing back to normal, studying them between the holidaymakers and honeymooners and strollers tied with balloons. The woman was blonde and slim, not unattractive under her sad eyes. The man was older, he noticed, whereas she looked around thirty-five—the age, he guessed, where she might be starting to panic about never having children. Had the child she'd longed for turned out to be someone else's?

His eyes flicked over their clothes. Both of them had the kind of grooming that took money. Maybe she'd been honest about not wanting his—it looked as if they had plenty of their own to go around. Of course, he rationalised, at the rates the Carmichael Clinic charged, they would have to have money.

It all seemed to fit.

'What do you think?' Simone prompted.

'Must be,' he mused, his eyes leaving the couple for a moment to scan the crowd. There were families and tourists and a gaunt-looking woman who looked as if she was lost in the crowd. No, there was nobody else it could be. He nodded, feeling a strange tightening in his chest as he contemplated this next step, twenty-four hours' notice strangely nowhere near enough to prepare himself to meet the woman carrying his child. 'Let's go find out.' He'd barely got the words out when the woman suddenly cried out and jumped to her feet.

The man followed, trying to placate her. Dominic cut a swathe through the pedestrian traffic. Did the woman think he wasn't going to show? He shouldn't have hesitated. Who else could it be? She was arguing through her sobs, her head turned back to the man holding her hand when he reached them.

'Mrs Cameron?'

'Mr and Mrs Pirelli?'

The couple looked around, both of them stunned for a moment, but Dominic's attention had already been snagged by the woman who'd arrived from left field, the woman with his name on her lips.

'Who are you?' he demanded.

CHAPTER THREE

SHE was shabby and pale, a ghost of a woman dressed in drab clothes and with hair the colour of dishwater pulled into an unkempt ponytail. Even as he took her in she seemed to shrink before him, her focus over his shoulder on the couple behind. 'I thought… I thought that was Mr and Mrs Pirelli.'

'I am Dominic Pirelli.'

'Oh.'

Simone came up alongside him with a click of heels and a whiff of that French perfume. 'Then you must be Mrs Cameron.'

Dominic wanted to argue the point. What did Simone think she was saying? He'd already decided who Mrs Cameron was and it wasn't this ragged excuse for a woman. Mrs Cameron was right here next to him—he swivelled around to see the couple rapidly disappearing into the crowd—and turned back, still not wanting to believe it could be true. How could this woman, this dishrag of a woman, be capable of carrying his child?

How could the clinic possibly have put his child into her?

But she was here, where they were supposed to meet, and she had uttered his name…

The shabby woman swallowed, and Dominic followed

the movement down a neck so thin it looked too small for her head. 'That's right,' she uttered, almost as if she were afraid of the admission. 'I'm…I'm Angie Cameron.'

Her voice cemented it as much as her admission. Unsure. Afraid. Sounding more like that teenager again when she must be—he peered at her, trying to put an age to her appearance—and failed. She looked nothing like the women he was used to dealing with in his life. For a woman so undernourished, she looked—weighed down.

'And you,' the ragged urchin offered, wiping her palms on her jeans before she held out her hand, 'must be Mrs Pirelli. I'm really sorry we have to meet in such circumstances.'

Her words were unnecessary. Dominic could not possibly imagine meeting her in any other. 'Simone is not my wife,' he said sharply. 'Simone is my PA.'

Something flickered in the PA's eyes at her boss's rapid fire correction, vanishing just as quickly, the brief touch of her fingers just as cool as the smile in her newly resumed demeanour. Angie blinked, way out of her depth, still reeling from making a fool of herself by approaching the wrong couple without being faced with this man—the man she'd decided could not possibly be the one. And now the woman with him was not his wife.

She could barely keep up.

She turned to offer her hand to the man but caught how he was looking at her—as is she were some kind of scum—and thought better of it, pulling her hand back.

Besides, even if she hadn't felt his revulsion, she wasn't sure she could cope with having her hand swallowed up in his. He'd looked tall from a distance before, but now, standing before her, he might well have been a mountain. Tall and broad-shouldered and composed entirely of rugged angles and treacherous planes. An insurmountable obstacle that she sensed with just one touch would drain her of what little strength she had.

No way would she risk that. Not when she needed every bit she did have for the tiny scrap of a baby growing inside her.

She closed her eyes. Oh, God. *This man's baby.*

A sudden gust of wind caught her and she swayed with it, stumbling a little before a manacle closed around her arm. But when she opened her eyes it was his hand that encircled her arm, his long fingers overlapping with the thumb. 'Sit down,' he growled, his deep voice all rough edges that rippled down her spine, 'before you fall down.'

He steered her backwards to the now empty seat and she collapsed gratefully onto it, still stunned that something made of skin and bone could feel like iron against her flesh. She put one hand to the place, sure she could feel the heat of his grip in the tingling band of skin.

He said something to the woman beside him, who disappeared efficiently in a click of heels and a flick of her hair while he looked around, raking the fingers of one hand through his hair. 'Where is your husband?' he asked, searching the crowd. 'Surely he came with you?'

'No. He's not here.'

His head swung back in disbelief. 'He made you come alone? In this condition?'

She almost managed to find a smile, certain he wasn't referring to her pregnancy, but then she remembered the look in his eyes—as if she were the lowest of the low—and any thoughts of smiling departed. She knew she looked like rubbish lately. Hadn't Shayne told her plenty of times? So instead she shrugged. 'It's hardly terminal. I get a little morning sickness. It passes by lunch time.'

Or it usually did. Today being the exception, of course. 'And then it was a mad dash from the station.'

The woman reappeared, holding a bottle of spring water. 'Here,' she said, holding it out. 'You look like you could do with this.'

Angie thanked her and unscrewed the cap, genuinely grateful for the gesture even if she hadn't needed yet another reminder of how bad she looked. The water was cool against her throat, refreshing both heated body and scrambled mind, opening the door to hope again. Maybe now the worst was over and there would be no more shocks. Maybe now they could just deal with the situation and get on with their lives.

'Have you eaten anything?'

'I'm not hungry,' she insisted, just wanting to get on with it and make the arrangements that needed to be made. But her stomach had other ideas, rumbling so loud there was no way she could hide it, and she cursed a fickle stomach that could be threatening to turn one moment and suddenly so desperately hungry that it felt as if it was about to devour itself in the next.

'Of course you're not hungry. Simone, go and find us a table at Marcello's. As private as possible. We'll be right along.'

'Are you sure? I thought you wanted somewhere public.'

'We can't talk here. Besides, this woman needs to eat.'

'Of course,' she said with a tight smile, though the look she flashed at Angie made it clear that she wasn't impressed. Then she flicked her head around and marched briskly off, her shiny bob swinging from side to side.

'I don't want to cause any fuss,' she said, her eyes on the departing woman, momentarily mesmerised by the movement in the sleek curtain of hair, knowing that the cut must have cost a fortune. She couldn't remember the last time she'd been to the hairdresser instead of cutting her hair herself in front of the bathroom mirror.

'Can you walk? Do you need help?'

She looked up at him and caught that look in his eyes again, as if he was weighing her up and assessing her suitability to bear his child and finding her wanting. Tough. He was stuck with her and she was stuck with him and they'd just have to make the best of it. She pushed herself to her feet, determined to show him that she didn't spend her entire day being blown around by gusts of wind. Or men who looked like mountains, for that matter. 'Thank you, but that won't be necessary. Neither will lunch. I'd rather just work out what we're going to do about this situation we happen to be in.'

'We can talk about "this situation" when you've had some sustenance. It will be easier to talk then,' he said, taking her forearm to steer her in the direction Simone had disappeared, sending a burst of shooting stars up her arm as she made to follow him. Instinctively she jerked her arm away, but he had already released her and she wondered if it was because he'd felt that same unexpected zing of current. But no. Far more likely that he'd simply achieved what he'd set out to do—he'd bossed her into submission and he could let her go, mission accomplished.

But she was too hungry to argue any more, too prepared to find the logic in his argument as she fell into step beside him. She needed to eat and they needed to talk. She'd probably have enough in her purse for a sandwich or something—anything to distract her from the strange tingling sensations under her skin. Like pins and needles except on the inside.

'Did I hurt you?'

She glanced up to find him watching her without breaking stride. 'Your arm,' he said. And only then did she realise she was absently rubbing the spot he'd held her.

'No,' she said, looking away from his penetrating gaze, suddenly afraid he might see too much. What was it about this man that he made her so uncomfortable? Because she knew he didn't like what he saw? Because he so clearly resented having to have anything to do with her? Well, that was his problem, not hers. And yet still she was the one who felt as skittish as a wild rabbit.

'Good,' he said, without glancing down at her. Not that he had to worry about looking where he was going. The crowd before them seemed to part in front of his purposeful stride, clearing a path for him to sweep majestically through, leaving her to wonder what kind of man he was, that he could part crowds with the sheer force of his presence. 'You're so thin I was worried I'd broken something. At least I know you will not be getting back on that train without having had something decent to eat.'

So now she was so thin she might snap? She told herself it really didn't matter a damn what he thought of how she looked and what she weighed. It wasn't as if they even had to like each other. Because after this baby was born, they'd probably never see each other again. After today if he'd prefer it. Yet still, his tone stung. She wasn't perfect by any means—she knew that more than anyone—but she'd be as good a mother for this child as she could possibly be in the months it was in her care. What more could anyone ask?

And then she wondered about his absent wife. Why had he brought his PA to this meeting instead of his wife? Surely she'd be curious.

Unless she'd been too upset by the news to come?

Or maybe he hadn't even told her yet?

Maybe he'd organised this meeting to vet her, to make sure she was actually worthy of carrying their child before breaking the news to his wife.

She stole a glance up at his compelling profile, at the strong blade of nose and sculpted angles of his jaw and suspected Mr Pirelli might be just that ruthless. And if today had been a test, then she had failed. His contemptuous looks were enough to make it clear she simply didn't make the grade.

She pulled her cardigan tighter around her shoulders, too hot beneath it even with the breeze whipping off the harbour, but needing the camouflage over arms that felt unusually thin. Then again, could she blame him if he was trying to protect his wife? How would she feel if their situations were reversed? Wouldn't she want the woman carrying her child to at least look human rather than some hollow-eyed stick insect? She'd stopped weighing herself lately. Her doctor had assured her she'd put on weight and look more like her old self as soon as the morning sickness stage passed but lately she was beginning to wonder if that would ever happen.

'Up here,' he said, gesturing towards a flight of steps leading inside, his fingers brushing past her elbow and sending another unwanted jolt of electricity up her arm that made her pulse race.

God, but she was jumpy! She hugged her tote closer to her side, pulling her elbows in as she climbed and making sure she kept her distance. Maybe it would be better if they didn't have to meet again after today. She didn't know how much of Dominic Pirelli her nerves could withstand.

But her nerves felt no better when she realised the stairs led away from the crowded tourist areas and food courts into an arcade spilling with gilded shops. It was quieter up here, the tone more exclusive. Without him by her side there was no way she'd ever venture up those stairs. They passed galleries displaying native art of dot paintings and carvings, and jewellery shops with windows filled with fat, lustrous pearls along with boutiques the likes of which she'd never have the courage to enter.

Beyond it all lay an intimate restaurant entrance. On the wall outside, the restaurant's name was spelled out in florid letters of burnished gold. *Marcello's*. They might just as well have spelled out the word *expensive*. Her footsteps slowed, despite the alluring scents coming from inside. He had to be kidding. She'd been thinking a quick sandwich, but this was a world away from the fast-food–type restaurants she was familiar with.

She stopped so suddenly he was halfway inside before he noticed. 'I can't go in there!' she said as he backed up, one eyebrow raised impatiently in question. 'Look at me.' She held out her arms and cast her eyes over her faded top and jeans. Had he forgotten the way he'd looked at her when he'd sized her up before? 'I shouldn't be here. I'm not dressed to eat out, let alone in a place like this!'

'It's no big deal.'

'They probably won't even serve me.'

'You're with me,' he said bluntly, making no concession to her ego by telling her she looked fine. 'They'll serve you.'

She shifted nervously. Did she really have to spell it out? 'The thing is, I didn't bring…' She hesitated, not wanting to reveal the sad truth of her finances even if it would probably come as no surprise. 'Look, I can't afford to eat in a place like this.'

He didn't blink. 'My treat. Ask for anything on the menu.'

'You're kidding? Anything?'

'Anything at all.'

Her stomach applauded with another growl, her resolve wavering even though she resented being made to feel like some kind of charity case. It was no contest. Forget haircuts, she told herself, already imagining the dishes to which those amazing scents belonged—she could cut her hair in front of the mirror for ever and she wouldn't care. But when was the last time she'd eaten out? Really eaten out in a proper restaurant, not a takeaway outlet? And in a surge of emotion she remembered.

Christmas, five years ago.

The Christmas just before her mother had died…

Hormones combined with harrowed nerves combined with dusty memories, resulting in a spontaneous rush of tears as she remembered a day that had broken her heart and set her on a collision course with disaster. 'Damn,' she said, brushing away the sudden moisture. 'I'm sorry. Thank you.'

'Don't read too much into it,' he said thickly. 'It's the baby I'm worried about.'

The door to her memories snapped shut. Arrogant man! Did he really think her tears were out of gratitude? Did he fear she was about to fall to the floor and kiss his feet or was he worried that she might possibly imagine he might be concerned for her welfare?

Not a chance!

She stiffened her spine and drew herself up to her full five feet eight. 'Tell me something I don't know, Mr Pirelli.' She swept past him in her faded jeans and chain store cardigan with as much dignity as she could muster.

Hadn't he already made it crystal clear with his un-veiled disdain that she was some kind of lesser being? She was under no misapprehension at all that he actually wanted to dine with her. His only concern was to make sure she ate something in order to nourish his precious baby.

Fine. But, baby or not, she was determined to enjoy every mouthful.

Her bravado lasted as long as it took to be noticed by the maître d', who with just one withering look managed to remind her who and what she was. Then he noticed who she was with and instantly he seemed to forgive her unseemly intrusion. He smiled widely, opening his arms in greeting. 'Signor Pirelli, it is always a pleasure to welcome you and your guests to Marcello's. This way, please.'

Angie tried to make herself as unobtrusive as possible as she followed in the men's wake. Except, she discovered, it was impossible to be unobtrusive when you were with the likes of Dominic Pirelli. Heads turned. Women who looked as if they'd been dressed by the boutiques they'd passed outside threw hungry glances his way, their eyes greedily devouring him, before turning to her, eyebrows rising, clearly wondering at the mismatch. She bowed her head and stared at the rich red carpet so she didn't have to read their expressions, but nothing blocked out the ripple of conversation and the titter of laughter that marked their progress through the room.

Her cheeks burned. Everyone knew she didn't belong here. Everyone, it seemed, but Mr Pirelli. Or maybe he just didn't care.

Their table was set in a private room, tucked discreetly away from all the others and boasting a wall of windows that gave an unrivalled view over the sparkling water below and caught her attention.

'Madam?' And she realised the maître d' was waiting, holding out a chair obviously intended for her and again she wished desperately they could have gone somewhere more casual, somewhere that had swivelling white plastic stools bolted to the floor like she was used to. She swallowed and sat, reaching for her serviette in relief when she hadn't managed to disgrace herself, unravelling its skilful folds only to realise another waiter was performing some kind of artful flick and drape into laps with the others. His hand hovered momentarily over the empty place hers should have been and she shrank down, wanting to hide. She did so not belong here in this upmarket world where even the waiting staff made her feel inferior.

Even the menu offered no respite, written entirely in Italian, so that she understood only the odd word. There were no prices. Angie blinked, mentally trying to work out how much eating here would cost. She'd been wrong in thinking it merely expensive. Diners here probably had to take out a mortgage.

And yet he came here often enough to be personally welcomed by the maître d'? How much money did he have that he could do that, let alone invite someone to eat here and not blink? What kind of work did this man do?

She looked longingly out of the window where ferries left white trails as they ploughed their way across the harbour and pleasure craft took a more leisurely approach, the moving vista a feast for the eyes, laid out beyond the glass like one more sumptuous course.

'We're in a hurry today, Diego,' she heard him say. 'Mrs Cameron has a train to catch.'

She turned in time for his nod. 'I understand. Would you like to order now, in that case?'

'Just my usual salad,' the other woman said.

'What would you like, Mrs Cameron?'

And she was faced with the question she'd been dreading ever since she'd looked at the menu. She was half tempted to say she would have the same as Simone except the only thing she did know was that a salad wasn't going to do it for her. She needed something entirely more substantial if she was going to soothe the savage beast inside her any time soon. She looked up at the waiter uncertainly. 'I don't suppose you happen to do steak?'

Simone smirked. The waiter blinked.

'The osso buco, I think,' Dominic said, taking her menu and passing them both to the waiter. 'Good choice. It'll be quick. Make that two.'

She nodded dumbly, thankful beyond measure for his intervention and knowing that whatever he'd ordered, she'd eat it. And at least it didn't sound like a salad.

'Did you have far to travel?' he asked.

'Not too far. Just out to Sherwill.'

'All that way?' Simone said as if she'd said she'd come from outer space. 'But that's halfway to Perth! Why would anyone live all the way out there?'

Because it's cheap, Angie thought, even if it is nasty with it, fully aware that everyone in Sydney would know of the outer western suburb given it featured on the nightly news so frequently. 'It's only an hour on the express.' When the trains were running to time.

Dominic scowled, no doubt racking up another black mark against her, courtesy of the area where she lived. And then he surprised her. 'Simone, I think I can handle it from here. You might as well go back to the office.'

'But Dom, surely you need minutes?'

'We'll manage. See you back at the office.'

Dismissed, the other woman had no choice but to leave as a waiter appeared bearing crusty bread and sparkling water. Angie fell upon both gratefully. The bread was dense and chewy and divine when slathered with butter so good it must be real, the sparkling water cool and refreshing.

She was still chewing when two waiters swept in bearing steaming plates of food and for a moment Angie was too staggered by the sight in front of her to think straight. There were mountains of meat in a rich tomato and vegetable sauce over an equally generous serving of golden rice. It looked and smelt fantastic and nothing like the steak she'd been expecting.

'This is what I ordered?'

'Osso buco,' Dominic said, as his own plate descended in front of him. 'It's actually veal, rather than steak. I think you'll like it.'

'It smells fantastic.'

'It's a classic Italian dish,' he said, picking up his fork. 'Do you like Italian food?'

'I don't know,' she said honestly, contemplating her plate, wondering where to start. Shayne had never been one for anything fancy or spicy, so she'd given up experimenting long ago. And at least it hadn't cost a lot to keep them in sausages and mash.

'Try it,' he prompted.

She didn't need her knife, she discovered; the meat fell apart with just her fork. She gathered a piece together with some of the sauce and rice, and lifted it to her mouth and tasted it, sighing with contentment as the flavours hit her tongue. It was divine, the meat so tender it practically melted in her mouth, the sauce rich and tasty, the rice golden with butter and tangy cheese.

'It's delicious,' she said, and then stopped, staggered to see what looked almost like a smile. It was so amazing the difference that one tiny tweak of his lips made to his face, transforming him from chiselled rock to flesh and blood in an instant. And suddenly he didn't just look powerful. He looked almost—real.

Devastatingly real.

And then he realised she was staring and the scowl returned.

'Eat up,' he ordered, the hard lines of his face back in control. 'And then we'll talk.'

He couldn't believe how much she could eat. Simone would have poked and prodded and chased around bits of tuna in her salad and still left half of it sitting in her bowl, whereas this woman had devoured—no, *demolished*—her entire plateful, as if it was the first decent meal she'd had in years. Then again, maybe it was, given the way the woman was now reaching for the bread to mop up the gravy. He couldn't remember the last time he'd seen a woman even eat bread, come to think of it. But then he'd never seen any woman eat like this one.

At least he knew that she wouldn't be going home hungry. More to the point, his baby wouldn't go hungry tonight.

His baby. Even twenty-four hours on, the very concept

still sent a shudder through his veins, the news so unexpected and left-field he was still having trouble trying to assimilate it.

Once upon a time he'd prayed for it to happen, if only so he could see Carla smile again and know that she meant it, if only so that she might finally find that elusive happiness she sought.

But the whole IVF process had been so intense, so clinical, and as it turned out, so laden with despair and disappointment that it had been a relief when the doctors had put a stop to it. He'd written off his chances of having a child then.

That it should happen now, so many years later, was a victory as bitter as it was sweet.

Because by some freakish accident, by some cruel twist of fate, he was going to be a father after all.

It had finally happened.

But why—damn it all, why—in the womb of this woman?

Cruel twist of fate?

Or cruel joke?

He screwed up the napkin in his lap, dropped it next to his plate. Cruel either way. *Because the one thing she had in common with Carla was the one thing he'd hated about her the most.*

God, and Dr Carmichael had assured him she was healthy. She didn't look healthy. And hadn't she practically fainted on him earlier? She was gaunt, her arms perilously thin and when she'd taken off her sunglasses to come inside, the dark circles under her eyes had threatened to swallow up her whole face.

And right now a niggling concern tugged at the edges of his admiration for her appetite. For there had been those rare times that Carla too had eaten well, getting his hopes up that maybe she was recovering, only for her to spend the next few hours locked in the bathroom purging herself of every last calorie.

He watched the woman opposite put down her knife and fork and take a sip of water. Any second now, he thought, the past flooding back with bitter clarity, she'll excuse herself...

But, instead, she surprised him by sitting back in her chair with a look of utter contentment on her face. 'That was amazing,' she said. 'I am so full.'

He might have smiled in other circumstances, if he hadn't already been counting. He knew the drill. Twenty minutes would be enough for her body to absorb vital nutrients for his child. He just had to keep her sitting there for twenty minutes.

The plates were cleared away, an order for coffee taken. The woman stuck with water though she'd been offered decaf. She made no attempt to go to the bathroom. He didn't like that he couldn't find fault with either of those things, even though there was an abundance of things about her that still rankled, from the way her hands fidgeted when she wasn't eating to the fact that this meeting was even necessary. But it was her appearance that was right up there near the top of the list.

Though he had to concede she looked better for eating. There was colour in her face now, he noticed, her cheeks faintly blushed, her lips pink and wide and surprisingly lush now that he thought about it. Strange, how much difference colour made to her features. Even her eyes seemed to have found colour somewhere, maybe because her face was no longer dominated by the dark circles under her eyes. Clear blue, like crystal clear pools where you could almost see the bottom but for the ripples on the surface, they looked almost too big for the rest of her face. He searched them now, wishing the ripples away so he could find out what it was that motivated her, what had really brought her here today, but they chose that moment to skitter away and he was left wondering—was she hiding something?

There was only one way to find out. 'Okay,' he said, placing a small voice recorder on the table between them, 'let's get down to business.'

Angie licked her lips. A moment ago she'd been enjoying the afterglow of the best meal she'd ever had, her tastebuds still tingling, alive with new flavours. But that was then. Now she felt his resentment coming in waves across the table and she didn't understand why. His tone and his words made it sound as if they were in the midst of some kind of business meeting rather discussing the future of the child she carried. 'What's that for?'

'For the record, Mrs Cameron. Rest assured, you'll be given a copy.'

She blinked. 'You don't trust me.'

His eyes pinned her across the table and for the first time she noticed just how dark they were, as dark as his voice was deep, as if they'd both been tapped from the same dark cavern, deep below the earth. 'Who said anything about not trusting you?'

Was he kidding? His answer was right there in his eyes, if not in his actions. 'But you don't trust me. You only bought me lunch because you couldn't trust me to eat it otherwise.'

Across the table he sat back hard against his seat back, the movement unwittingly drawing her eyes to the pull of fine, crisp cotton against broad masculine chest, a random thought approving of the contrast of white cotton against the olive skin at his open neck. 'Put it this way,' he said, and she blinked, annoyed with herself that she'd been distracted. She had no business noticing such details. She didn't *want* to notice such things. Certainly not about him.

'The thing is,' he continued, 'I don't know you, and you don't know me. And, even if we did know each other, given the fact it's months until this child is born, I think it's wise to ensure from the beginning there are no misunderstandings down the track. Don't you?'

'What kind of misunderstandings?'

He shrugged, no casual shrug but a deliberate and calculated movement of those broad shoulders. This time she didn't allow her eyes to linger longer than to get the impression that he would just as easily shrug her off, if only he could. 'Either one of us could say things today and then change their mind before the baby is born.'

'I'm not changing my mind!'

'Then you have nothing to worry about.'

'And you don't need the recording.'

'No?' He leaned forward. 'But what if I were to change my mind? Trust works both ways, Mrs Cameron.'

If he changed his mind? Angie sat back in her chair, her fingers knotting in her lap, her fingertips finding the absent place where her rings had once been. He was messing with her head, talking trust and misunderstandings. She'd assumed she'd turn up today and he'd agree to take the baby. It was that simple.

Wasn't it?

'So what you're actually telling me, Mr Pirelli, is that you're not a man to be trusted.'

Even as his mouth curved into a smile, one look at his cold, glittering eyes and Angie realised she'd just overstepped some unseen line. 'Like I said,' he clarified in that deep voice that seemed to rumble its way through her very bones like the growl of a jungle cat and sounded just as ominous, 'we don't know each other. And this is no stray cat or a dog we're talking about. This is a child. *My child*. A baby that won't be born for six months. You think I'm going to leave that to chance? I want whatever we decide on paper. I want it watertight. And I don't want there to be any chance that one of us can change our minds. Not where this baby is concerned.'

She sighed, dropping her head into her hands. This was so not how she'd imagined this meeting going. But maybe she'd been naive in thinking this would be simple. Maybe he was right. For it wasn't as if they were talking about a puppy that had wandered into the wrong house that she was returning. It was a baby, a child that had been implanted into the wrong woman and which wouldn't be born for six long months. Of course they would need some kind of record of their agreement. 'Okay,' she conceded, 'we'll do it your way.'

'Good,' he said, impatience more than satisfaction weighing down the word as he leaned forward to switch the machine on. 'Let's get on with it. First to the basics. You're currently approximately twelve weeks pregnant with a child that is not your own, is that so?'

'That's right.'

'After being mistakenly implanted with my biological child rather than your own embryo.'

She nodded, adding a late, 'Yes.'

'And you called me yesterday to tell me this.'

'Yes.'

'And why did you do that, Mrs Cameron? What is it you're proposing, exactly?'

Was he kidding? 'I'm having your baby, Mr Pirelli. And I'm here now. What do you think I'm proposing?'

'You're the one who called. You tell me.'

'Okay.' She sucked in a breath tinged with frustration. Hadn't they been through this? 'The way I see it, this baby growing inside me is not my child. I thought that you would want to know about it. And I was hoping that maybe, just maybe, you might actually want the child once it is born.'

'Because you don't?'

He made it sound like an accusation. She didn't want any baby. Not really. But that was none of his business. 'This baby is yours. I thought—I hoped—that you'd want it.'

'So you're saying you're prepared to have this baby and hand it over?'

'Of course.'

'As soon as it's born?'

'It would be difficult to do it any earlier.' Across the table, a jaw clenched, tightening to rock and dark eyes glittered ominously, warning her this was no joking matter. But what did he expect? He was the one turning this meeting into an inquisition. 'Of course that's what I'm saying! That's why I'm here. This child, this baby, has nothing to do with me. Not really.'

'So you would hand over this child and walk away, and expect to have nothing to do with it ever again?'

'Why would I want to when it's not my child?'

He leaned forward. 'You see, that's what I'm having trouble understanding, Mrs Cameron. Why would you carry through with this pregnancy when it is not your child?' Dark eyes caught menacingly in the downlights, gleaming dangerously as he leaned across the table towards her. 'Unless there's something you're expecting in return?'

CHAPTER FOUR

ANGIE blinked, her heart racing, her mind scrambling to keep up. 'I have no idea what you mean.'

'Oh, come on. You expect me to believe you're making some kind of altruistic gesture out of the goodness of your heart and that you'll hand this baby over and expect nothing in return? Nothing? Why don't you just come clean? How much are you asking?'

She shook her head. He'd asked her yesterday over the phone what was in it for her, but she'd figured it was a knee-jerk reaction, born of shock. She'd never imagined he really believed it of her. 'This has nothing to do with money.'

His expression darkened with disbelief, his eyes raking over her and making no attempt to disguise his scorn. 'Come on, Mrs Cameron. You're expecting me to believe you couldn't do with a little extra cash?'

He was actually serious. Okay, so maybe she could do with some extra cash and it showed. But there was no need for him to sit there, looking so smugly imperious, like a Roman emperor ready to toss some scraps to a waiting pleb. She didn't want his scraps. She didn't want anything of his.

Ever again.

But some perverse part of her insisted she play his

game. Maybe he was right. Maybe she should be asking for money if he was so very keen to force it on her. The clinic had promised to cover all her medical expenses, but Shayne had given her nothing in maintenance and her little nest egg wouldn't last for ever now she'd lost her job. And that perverse little voice asked if it would be so very wrong to ask, given he seemed so keen to part with his money. 'So what exactly are you offering?'

Nothing about him moved, save for his lips that turned into a half smile, and she tried to ignore the feeling that she'd just made some terrible mistake and wondered whether there was any chance she could make it right if she had.

'Inconvenience money,' he offered, watching her intently now, 'given what you're undertaking and given your own plans for a child have been delayed. Surely you must be anxious to try again.' He was sure he had her now. Her point-blank denials had been frustrating him but they hadn't lasted long until she'd been the one to ask what was on offer. It had been the crack he'd been waiting for. Nobody would do what she was doing for nothing, and with that lapse she'd proven it. He waited while she stared at the glass in her hand, waited while she weighed up his words, wondering if already she was counting the dollar signs; wondering if she even realised she was worrying that bottom lip of hers with her white teeth. The gesture spoke of an innocence he knew she couldn't possibly possess. Yet still he found himself unable to look away.

And then she looked up and met his gaze. 'Look, that's actually very sweet of you, Mr Pirelli,' she said, 'but my next pregnancy is my business. And I've decided I can wait.'

He couldn't believe what he was hearing, not when

he'd thought he had her, now when she'd been the one to ask what was on offer. He cursed himself for insisting on the recording device. It had to be what had made her so reluctant before and what was inhibiting her now. But he wasn't about to give up yet. 'What about your husband—what does he think?'

She looked anxiously around, and he wondered if she was looking for a waiter. But no, her water was still full so it couldn't be that. 'He…he's happy for me to handle this.'

'But surely he must be upset about this whole thing?'

She licked her lips, reaching for the glass. Not drinking, but just twirling the contents, as if searching for something to do and something else to focus on. 'We've come to an agreement.'

'What kind of agreement?'

Her glass stopped twirling. Her eyes snapped up. 'The kind of agreement that's between Shayne and me. The kind of agreement that doesn't concern you.'

'Doesn't it, given right now you're carrying my child?'

What did he want? Blood? She was sick of her motives being questioned when she was only here to offer him his baby. Had he never heard of the words *thank you*? 'Look, Mr Pirelli, do you actually want this baby or not? Only there's an adoption list a mile long.'

'This baby will not be adopted!'

'Fine. But you're lucky there's even going to be a baby, given what the clinic offered!'

Cold hard silence descended over the table. Like a blanket of fog, it chilled the atmosphere and set his face to stone.

'What did the clinic offer?'

She cursed the impulse that had made her lash out at him, cursed the words that had issued from her mouth when she'd never had any intention of acting upon them. But maybe he needed to hear them. Maybe then he would appreciate what she was trying to do. She swallowed, her throat almost too tight to get out the words. 'They suggested I have an abortion. Cover the whole thing up quietly. Without you ever knowing.'

Skin pulled tight over cheekbones, the cords of his throat stood out rigid and tight, a throbbing pulse at his temple, and she was suddenly back in her dream, the snarling dog closing in on her, its powerful shoulders bringing it ever closer until she could almost feel its hot angry breath against her face. Was this the man she'd imagined in her nightmare? Was this man the snarling danger in the dark?

'I said no!' she insisted, shaken by the return of the images in her nightmare. 'Obviously, I said no.' It had never been an option as far as she was concerned.

'Obviously, you said no,' he echoed, the words sounding as if they'd been ground out of all the dark, jagged places inside him. 'Because you realised this baby was worth more to you alive. You decided you could sell it instead.'

'No! You honestly believe I could sell this baby—your baby—back to you? What kind of person do you think I am?'

'I don't know what kind of person you are, Mrs Cameron. I don't know why anyone would want to willingly bear someone else's child—a stranger's child. Why would they do that, if not for money, when you are clearly on the bones of your arse.'

It was too much! She stood shakily to her feet, sick of his mistrust, sick of his constant references to how pitiable she was. 'Just like you said, Mr Pirelli, you don't know me. You don't know me at all. And clearly I made a mistake coming here. I thought you'd be interested in raising your own child, but I can see now that all you're worried about is your money. And it seems to me that this child would be much better off being raised as far away from you as humanly possible. Thank you for lunch. I'm leaving.'

She swung her tote over her shoulder even as his voice boomed out across the table. 'You're not going anywhere!' His hand caught the swinging bag and sent it crashing to the floor, throwing its contents across the carpet.

'Now look what you've done,' she cried as she surveyed her scattered possessions—the folded train time-table, her old comb with its broken teeth, the cheap mascara and lipstick she hadn't felt well enough to apply today, and what was left of the bottle of water his PA had given her—and knelt down to collect everything, until she lifted the now empty bag and, with a sickening lurch to her heart, realised something was missing. 'Where's my wallet?'

There was no wallet. 'Are you sure you had it?' he asked with a hand under her elbow to lift her, his touch still tripping her nerves in a way she was now convinced was caused by making contact with the force field of his resentment.

'I know I had it!' But with a thud she remembered the man who'd shoved into her as she was coming off the train, nearly sending her sprawling, before rushing off into the crowd. She looked up at him. 'Someone pushed me getting off the train. I thought it was an accident, but do you think…?'

She'd gone from spitting she-cat to victim again,

looking so devastated and ashen he was worried she was going to faint again. He steered her back down into her seat and pulled his mobile phone from his pocket, dialling the police and cursing the scumbag who would steal from someone who clearly didn't have two cents to rub together. 'How much was in it?'

'More than twenty dollars!' And then she paused, shocked. 'Oh, God, and my train ticket.' She looked up at him, her eyes already spilling over with tears. 'I'm sorry. I realise you hate me and I know I said some awful things just now, but do you think you could loan me the money for the fare home?'

Alongside him in the passenger seat she said nothing. He didn't prompt her, he didn't try to fill in the silence. They'd said enough over lunch.

She'd surprised him with that outburst. He'd assumed from her appearance that she lacked passion. He'd assumed any personality was as lacklustre as her appearance. But instead of the admission he'd been expecting in response to his goads, she'd simply turned around and given as good as she'd got. *The mouse that roared.*

Albeit only until the time she'd realised her purse had been snatched. Since then she'd returned to the land of the hapless and forlorn.

It must have nearly killed her to have to ask him for the fare home.

Angie sat back in the high-backed leather seat that seemed to wrap itself around her, the smell of fine leather and expensive car and expensive man all wending its way through her senses, and only wished she could enjoy the experience. The man alongside her made that impossible. She dared a glance in his direction, unable to stop herself from admiring the long-fingered hands resting on the wheel, the way they manoeuvred the car and the gear changes with complete assurance and control. Powerful hands, she thought, remembering the impact of their touch on her skin, powerful hands for a powerful man. Powerful and utterly ruthless.

And so sure she was after his money. She looked around at the car's interior, drank in the smell of leather upholstery and figured he must have plenty if this kind of car was his city runabout.

So why the hell was she fighting him? He already thought the worst of her. He'd made no attempt to deny that he hated her. Why not take his money? It wasn't as if she couldn't use it.

She squeezed her eyes shut. She'd been so naive! Shayne had walked out on her and she'd become so obsessed with finding this baby's parents, so consumed with ensuring its future was assured, that she hadn't stopped to consider her own. Shayne had walked out on her and her brain had shut down.

Of course she could do with the money. The mortgage on the house her mother had left her wasn't big, but she would need some kind of income in the coming months to meet the repayments and bills and keep her in groceries. Not to mention if she wanted to replace the furniture Shayne had taken with him any time soon.

Why had she made such a big deal of his offer?

Because of the way he'd framed it? As if she were some gold-digger out to make what she could by selling his own baby to him? Or because she was just sick of men expecting her to do what they wanted?

Maybe both.

He stole a glance at her profile, noticing her frown and the teeth worrying her lip again. She'd be worried about her stolen purse and how she was going to get by without the measly twenty bucks it contained, though to her twenty dollars probably seemed like a fortune.

Maybe he shouldn't have been so hard on her.

Maybe she was genuine.

Yeah, sure, and maybe this whole thing was one bad dream.

After all, hadn't she asked him what he was offering? What was that if not an admission of guilt?

His teeth ground together, gnawing on the problem, still not satisfied. So why had it taken so much effort on his part to get her to bite? What was her angle? She had to have one.

Because it was clear she would need money. The child in her womb should not go wanting for the next six months of its life merely because she was too proud or too foolish to accept his help. If she didn't want to ask for it, he would make her take it.

The Mercedes ate up the bitumen as it headed westwards past Parramatta on the long straight highway that he'd once known so well.

With every passing kilometre, his gut twisted tighter. With every passing kilometre, it felt as if the intervening years were peeling away. And with every landmark he recognised, it felt as if the past was sucking him further and further back, into a life he'd long thought forgotten. The highway was upgraded, the buildings more modern, but still the memories piled upon him until it felt as if he were drowning underneath them.

They passed the cheap second-hand car lot where he'd bought his first set of wheels. Even now, cosseted in the luxury of his Mercedes E-class Coupe, it was impossible not to remember the excitement of the youth who had scraped together the deposit on his first car.

It had been riddled with rust, had a dodgy clutch cable

and faulty lights but that car had signalled he was going places. And he had. Twelve months later he had moved on, never to return.

Not that he'd had any reason to. His grandparents had gone. His mother had gone. He'd left the past behind, neatly packaged in a box marked *Do Not Open*.

He mentally shoved the box aside lest he further disturb its dusty contents and stole another glance at the woman alongside him. She sat tense as a bowstring with her hands firmly clutched around the straps of her bag, as if she might somehow still protect the purse that was no longer there.

With her face angled away, he could just see the tilt of her nose, the high line of her cheekbones and the curve of her lips. And from this angle it occurred to him that she was almost pretty, in a sad, neglected kind of way. Or maybe she had been pretty once, but it had prematurely slipped away under a baking western suburbs sun and the constant battle to survive. But he'd be damned if he was going to let her merely survive for the next six months.

'I think we both know you're going to need my help with this baby.'

He was looking straight ahead, changing lanes in preparation for the turn he knew was coming up soon but still he was aware of the exact moment her eyes fell on him. Somehow he could feel their cool blue gaze washing over his skin.

'I know. I'm sorry. You're right.'

The simple declaration was the first surprise. The fact that she didn't argue the second. But it was the apology that surprised him even more, especially given the way he'd assumed the worst of her from the start.

'I want this child,' he said, his voice lacking the heat

that had been the hallmark of their earlier meeting but threaded with a steel-plated determination that surprised even him as he ground out the words. 'And I will not see you go without while you do this.'

In his peripheral vision he picked up her quaking nod. But it was more the sigh of acceptance he sensed that told him what she thought before she spoke. 'I'm so glad you want this baby.'

He half wondered why it was so important to her. But then, he didn't understand why this baby and what happened to it was so important to him. Once upon a time he'd been happy that Carla had never managed to conceive, resigned never to having children of his own because he was so angry with her and what she'd done to herself, so angry that she could have left a child motherless by virtue of her own self-destructive actions.

So why did he feel so strongly about it now?

Other than it was his child. It existed. It belonged with him.

And the woman alongside him was making that possible.

God, but he'd been hard on her. But he'd had to find out. Had to test her. 'I'll speak to my lawyers. There has to be some kind of precedent for this kind of thing. They'll work something out.'

He heard her breathe in. Wondered if she was going to argue again. Then she huffed out a wary, 'Thank you. Maybe that would be helpful.' Some new quality in her voice alerted him and, curious, he glanced her way. The frown was gone, from what he could see, her lip liberated from her teeth and, if he wasn't mistaken, there was almost the hint of a smile at her mouth.

He turned his eyes back to the road though his attention stayed firmly with what he'd witnessed. It was the

first time he'd seen her face come anywhere near a smile.
He wasn't entirely sure she knew how to. And while the
business part of his brain told him it was only because
he was insisting she take his money, his gut was not so
convinced.

Whatever the reason, the expression took years off
her.

He glanced again, not sure if he'd imagined it, and,
as if sensing his gaze, she looked around and for one
solitary moment as their eyes jagged and caught it was
still there on her lips, until she blinked, her eyes filling
with confusion as the smile slid away.

'Oh,' she said, jumping when she saw where they
were, 'you have to turn right at the next intersection,'
even though he was already in the slip lane indicating
for the turn.

What was happening to her? Angie pushed back in
her seat and took a deep breath, suddenly too warm
despite the air-conditioned interior. It was because of
his eyes, she realised.

Because for the first time he'd looked at her as if she
wasn't something he might find on the bottom of his
shoe. He'd looked at her as if he was actually seeing
her—the person—and it had thrown her, that was all.
Coming on top of learning that he definitely wanted this
child, of course it would throw her.

'Where exactly do you live?' he asked as the turning
lights went green.

She gave him the address, expecting him to ask her
for directions, surprised when he didn't, but he looked
so deep in thought as he drove—more than a mere frown
tugging at his brows—that she didn't offer. Besides,
there was plenty of time before the next turn.

'We'll have to meet again to sign some kind of

agreement,' he said a little while later, his rumbling voice sounding distant, and, when she turned to look at him, his gaze was still firmly fixed on the road ahead, his expression still tight. Even the fingers that until now had seemed so relaxed and composed on the steering wheel were curled tightly around it. And then he turned to her, blinking as he focused, and Angie got the distinct impression that while he'd been telling her one thing, his mind had been miles away. 'Don't worry,' he assured her. 'It will be drawn up to protect your interests too.'

She wasn't even sure what her interests would be but for some strange reason she trusted him. 'I understand.'

'Will your husband be able to join you next time?'

Shayne? She looked away, suddenly nervous again. 'Does he need to be there?'

'Of course. The way I understand it, as birth mother, this child will be legally yours, regardless of where the embryo originated. As your husband, any agreement to hand over the child will no doubt require Shayne's signature too.'

Angie's spirit slumped. Damn. Why—just when it looked as if things were going to work out—did something have to go wrong? How was she ever going to convince Shayne to help her with this when he'd been so opposed to what she was doing from the start? She sighed. She doubted he'd even take her call. 'I'll see what I can do.'

'If it's a problem, I can send out a car for you, so you don't have to catch the train.'

'You don't have to—'

'After what happened today, no more trains. It's not safe.' He looked across at her. 'Understood?'

'Now, hang on,' she started, her concerns about

Shayne giving way to irritation. No matter what they agreed between them about the future of this child, there was no way he could tell her how she was going to get from point A to point B. Especially since Shayne had taken the car when he'd gone. 'What if I don't have a car?'

'You don't?' He sounded incredulous, and then, in the next breath, took hers away.

'Then I will have one delivered tomorrow. I do not want you walking around this area either.'

'No! You can't—' But she didn't finish what she was going to say, not once she'd looked around and realised he'd taken the first two turns into her suburb without her telling him which way to go and was already signalling the turn into her street and pulling up alongside her house.

'How did you…' But he was already out of his seat and halfway around to her door.

She didn't wait for an explanation. She was already getting out of the car, determined to say her goodbyes here, before he got closer to her house. If he thought her pitiful already, what would he think if he knew the full extent of her pathetic circumstances? It was inevitable he'd find out some time—she could hardly keep it a secret for ever—but damned if she wanted him to find out today. She was too emotionally wrung out to take any more of his contempt today.

For a big man, though, he moved fast. She was barely out of her seat and he was there, hemming her in between her open door and the force field of his presence, blocking off the promise of escape.

'Thanks for the lift,' she said. 'Bye.' But he made no move to let her go and there was no stepping around the barrier he made with just his sheer physical presence.

'Maybe I can meet your husband now, if he's home.' It wasn't a question.

She clutched her bag to her chest, shook her head. 'He's not.'

An eyebrow arched in question. 'How can you be so sure?'

She looked longingly towards the house. It wasn't much to look at but it was almost all hers and right now she yearned for the sanctuary its walls would provide. 'He…he never gets home before five.' Though it had been closer to nine, she remembered with a touch of bitterness, before he'd walked out on her completely, claiming he was working overtime while all the time he'd been out with the new office assistant. How naive she'd been!

'Are you all right?' he asked, wondering at the tension around her eyes and mouth and the bright spots of colour in an otherwise pale face, worried she might be about to faint on him again.

'I'm fine,' she said, at odds with her increasingly edgy body language as she shifted nervously on the spot and tucked wayward tendrils of hair behind her ears. She was smiling, if you could call it that, her lips drawn tight, her eyes so falsely bright that he wondered again if she wasn't hiding something. 'Thanks again for the lift. I won't hold you up any longer.'

'I'll be in touch tomorrow,' he said, moving aside to let her pass, and within seconds she'd scooped the mail from her letterbox and was halfway across the dust-bowl of her front yard, the wave from one hand her only response.

He waited there while she let herself into the house, saw her look over her shoulder one last time before disappearing inside. Maybe she was just embarrassed. Looking at the house, he could understand why.

The building was low and squat, perched meanly over what had once been a lawn before soaring summer temperatures and water restrictions had killed it off. He knew exactly what the house would look like on the inside because there were street upon street of them, all with slightly different frontages, half with the driveway on the left, half on the right, but all based on the same two or three basic floor plans. He could still see it now. Just inside the front door would be a lounge room along with a rudimentary kitchen and bathroom. There would be three bedrooms, one slightly larger passing for the master bedroom, one half the size of that and just big enough for a single bed and chest of drawers. The third would be half that size again, no more than a storeroom really.

Even now, thirty years on, he remembered the feel of those walls pressing in around the dreams he'd dreamed in his small fold-out bed.

Even driving through the suburb made him feel claustrophobic—the very sameness of it all, the dreariness of design, the street after street of untended gardens and poorly maintained paintwork—almost as if whatever dream the occupants had once had, had died a slow and painful death.

He'd done well to escape it.

He'd worked damned hard to escape it.

Which made it all the more ironic that this was the first place his child would live. Thank God that, unlike him, it was never a place his child would experience first-hand.

But it didn't stop him feeling sick to the stomach at

the thought of leaving his child behind now. The birth could not come soon enough.

How many months to go?

How many months when she would be living in a suburb he'd sworn he would never set foot in again? He didn't even want to think about the danger of everyday life out here. Break-ins, school arson and street violence, the suburb made an art form of urban unrest. What kind of environment was that for his baby to develop in?

No kind at all. And it rankled that he should be given this gift of an unborn child, only to have to worry about whether mother and baby survived long enough for him to take the child.

Incubator and baby, he corrected himself as he turned the key in the ignition, the Mercedes purring into life. He couldn't actually bear to think of this woman as its mother.

It was wrong.

She might be pregnant with his child, but this woman was simply a caretaker for the next however months. She would never be his child's mother.

Never in a million years!

CHAPTER FIVE

ANGIE slumped against the closed front door, tension draining from her body as she sighed with relief. After what felt like the longest day of her life, after an impossibly draining few hours with an impossible man, finally she was free. Outside, she heard his car engine purr like a jungle cat into life, then the smooth sound of it accelerating away.

Another sigh of relief. He was gone.

And yet still she was unable to get the picture of man and machine out of her head. She shouldn't have looked. She'd tried to resist. But the temptation to steal just one more glance had been too much.

So she'd peeked over her shoulder and seen him standing there alongside that car of his, watching her, his arms crossed, his eyes shaded by dark glasses that may have covered his eyes but did nothing to hide the intensity of his expression.

So intense she'd had to catch her breath as sensation had skittered up her spine. The sleek black car looked like sin. Its owner had looked even more dangerous. More potent, reminding her of some of the ads in the motoring magazines Shayne had sometimes pored over, except the car would be positioned strategically at the very edge of a cliff top or on a highway next to a rolling surf beach, places that matched driver and machine for pure unbridled beauty. Not places like Spinifex Avenue, with its drab houses and front yards filled with dead gardens and rusting car bodies.

Whoever Dominic Pirelli was and wherever he came from, he did so not belong here.

With a sigh, she pushed herself away from the door and through the near empty lounge room to the kitchen. She dropped her bag on the table, snapped on the kettle and flicked through the mail while she waited for the water to boil. *Great.* All window envelopes—electricity, rates and... Her heart tripping faster in her chest as she recognised the name of the legal aid office Shayne was using. What did they want now? She tore open the envelope and pulled out the letter, scanning its contents, her mind refusing to believe what her eyes were telling her.

She collapsed onto one of the two remaining mis-matched chairs, gutted that he could do this to her. He'd already taken the car and most of the furniture. He'd told her he'd wanted nothing else but a divorce from her ever again.

She read the letter again, slower this time in spite of a heart beating like thunder that sent panic coursing around her body, but the words remained unchanged, their meaning starkly clear.

Shayne wanted a property settlement agreed as quickly as possible. Only now he was claiming half the house—the house that had been her mother's pride and joy, the house her mother had left her in her will. *Her house.*

And if he got that, there was no way she could pay

him out without selling and then where would she go? Where would she live?

What the hell was she supposed to do?

Dominic reached an intersection, knew he should turn right for the highway but inexplicably turned left instead, wending his way through streets marked with signs long past their use-by date. He didn't need them anyway. He'd escaped his past a long time ago, he'd thought, but his past was still there, buried deep inside that box, waiting for the opportunity to burrow its way out.

His heart hammering, he slowed as he passed a tired shopping centre where all the windows wore security grilles and where half the shops were empty, feeling a strange lurch in his gut to see the laundromat shabbier but still open for business. His mother had found him crying in there, hiding behind the row of machines, bleeding from the split in his ear where a rock had caught him and from where he'd slid on gravel and taken the skin off both knees. He'd been ashamed he'd run. Ashamed he'd been caught. But most of all he'd been ashamed he'd cried.

And right there on the floor of the laundromat, amidst the steam and the hum and clang of a dozen machines, his mother had hugged him tight and cried right along with him. She would make it better, she promised him. She would take him away from his horrible school and the bullies who hated anyone who was good at anything. She would buy them both a house by the sea like Nonna and Poppa always talked about buying, somewhere he could be happy.

And his tears had dried as she'd woven her magic promises and spun a golden future for them both that he would dream about every night in bed, just waiting for the day, because his mother worked so hard and he knew she would shift heaven and earth to make it happen.

The shopping centre fell behind, his car seemed to be on autopilot, unravelling the years as it wended its way through the suburb until he was there, crawling along the narrow street to number twenty-four, more afraid now of what he would remember than what he would find. He turned up the airconditioning, his palms sweaty against the wheel as he passed the tiny playground where his poppa had watched him play when his mother was working, his poppa busy carving a piece of wood he'd pull from his pocket. He remembered watching the shavings curl as he worked the tool through the wood, creating another tiny masterpiece. And he remembered running back to the house at dinner time, and the smell of rich tomato dishes that met him, and Nonna in the kitchen wearing a white apron and letting him stand on a chair and taste the minestrone from what seemed then like a massive wooden spoon.

And then he did a double take when he got to number twenty-four, or what was left of it, little more than a burned-out shell, the tiled roof caved in and with police tape still stuck between poles. He got out of the car and stood there on the side of the road, the air still tainted with the smell of ash and burning.

Gone. All gone now. His grandparents and the fragrant kitchen. His mother and her promises and dreams. Even the very house where he'd nursed her in her final weeks before the tumour that stopped her in her tracks had claimed her for its own.

All gone.

'You from the insurance company?' A grizzled old man wearing a white singlet and shorts stood watering a stringy row of tomato plants next door with a bucket, clearly more interested in the stranger with the flash car.

Dominic shook his head. 'What happened, do you know?' And the old man frowned as he looked at what was left of the house. 'Bad business. Some feud between some local school kids, barely out of primary school, not that they didn't know what they were doing. A gang of them came around and threw home-made Molotov cocktails through the windows. The wife and I heard the crash. By the time we came out to see what was happening, the place was going like a bonfire. Too quick for the firies.'

God. 'What about the people who lived here? Are they okay?'

'Yeah. How they made it out in time, I don't know. Single mum with a couple of kids. Another one on the way. A miracle they all made it out alive, we reckon.'

'She was pregnant.' He wasn't really asking. He was thinking, his eyes on the burned-out shell of the house where he'd grown up.

'Yeah. It's a miracle, all right.'

A miracle? It sounded more like hell on earth to him. What if this had happened three streets away? What if they'd got the wrong house? What if another woman wasn't fast enough to get out?

He imagined the fear the woman must have felt. Imagined the panic at the crash of windows and the heat from the flames and the desperation to get herself and her children out before they might succumb to the fire and the smoke. What kind of experience was that for anyone to go through, let alone a pregnant woman? Let alone her unborn child?

How could he now drive away and leave her here, exposed to who only knew what danger?

How could he calmly head home and leave his baby behind?

It wasn't going to happen.

Something else would have to be organised. An apartment. A six month lease. It would work. Now he just had to make them see that.

Angie was still at the kitchen table clutching the letter when the knock came, loud and purposeful. She jumped and swiped a tissue over her cheeks, mopping up what she could of her tears. What now? Was Shayne already sending around real estate agents to hasten the process?

The knock came again, more insistent this time. Whoever it was wasn't going away. She sniffed and stole a glance through the window, frowning when she saw a familiar-looking black car outside. Why was he back? Surely he hadn't changed his mind. Although the way this day was going...

She opened the door with the safety chain in place, just enough that they could talk through the crack, not enough that he could see into the empty lounge room within. But even the small sliver of him was enough to remind her of his sheer power and presence. She could feel his aura like a blanket of heat. 'What do you want?'

'Let me in. I have to talk to you.'

'What about?'

'You expect me to talk through a crack in the door? I'm not going to hurt you. I'm not about to mug the woman carrying my child.'

She sighed. Did it really matter if he found the truth

out now rather than later? There was no way she could hide the truth for ever. She pushed the door closed, released the safety chain and reluctantly opened her house to him, knowing it would inevitably result in baring her soul.

'I've got a proposal for you,' he said, oblivious to her discomfort as he strode past her, the woody tang of his masculine scent curling into her senses. She breathed it in, wondering how just a scent could convey a sense of power and luxury. 'When will your husband…'

He stopped, staring at the near empty room and she saw it through his eyes—the sole armchair and old television set, a rickety side table with a stack of library books on pregnancy and birth and a star-shaped ticking clock on the wall that had been there for ever.

He turned, slowly and purposefully. 'What the hell is going on? Is this how you live?' He peered closer at her face. 'Have you been crying?'

Lids fell shut over eyes that still felt scratchy raw. She prayed for strength. Because the disdain was back in his voice and his words and his body language. The censure was back. And if he offered her pity she'd have the whole damned trifecta.

'There was more furniture,' she said, avoiding the second part of his question.

'What did you do? Sell it to buy a tin of beans?'

No, damn it! She wheeled away. Headed for the kitchen. She was wrong. She couldn't do this now. She didn't need it.

She snapped the kettle on again, determined this time to have that cup of tea she'd promised herself, but then she turned to get the milk and he was right there, shrinking the kitchen with his height and those damned broad shoulders as he took in the boxes in one corner, stacked with crockery and glasses from the dresser Shayne had decided he'd like. 'Are you packing? Are you going somewhere?'

'No!' He was standing between her and the fridge. She gave up on the milk. Pulled a cup instead from a cupboard and dropped in a herbal tea bag. Stood there with her arms crossed and her back to him while the kettle roared back into life.

'Then do you want to tell me what the hell is going on?'

The roar from the kettle became a burble, the burble became a shrill thin whistle and her nerves stretched to breaking point.

'What are you trying to hide?'

She reached out a hand to turn it off but he caught it and spun her around so fast she was left breathless. Or maybe it was just the touch of his big hand around her wrist, the heat of his fingers imprinting on her flesh and the impact of six foot something of potent male standing within inches of her. 'Tell me!'

'Fine!' she said over the noise from the kettle. 'Shayne took the furniture, okay!'

'Why? Why would he take it?'

The kettle screamed, steam billowing in hot damp clouds around her. 'So he could shack up with his teen-age girlfriend. Why do you think? And now do you think I might turn that off?'

'Shayne's gone?' He let her go and stepped back as she turned and pulled the plug and the fever pitch screaming wound down. Pieces of the puzzle slipped into place—her unwillingness to talk about him, her circling the issue whenever he was mentioned, the fact she'd gone to their meeting today alone.

Because her jerk of a husband had left her for someone else. 'When did this happen?'

She shrugged, filled her cup with water and dunked her tea bag. He waited while she performed the action the requisite number of times before dropping the tea bag into the sink, where it landed with a splat. Then she turned and leaned back against the sink, cradling the cup in her hands. 'He moved in with his girlfriend two months ago.'

She could have been reciting a shopping list, her voice was so calm, belying the obvious trauma that underpinned her words.

Two months ago? How long had they known about the mix-up? Was it a coincidence? 'Why did he leave you?'

Her blue eyes turned misty and desolate as she stared into her tea. 'Because I refused to have the abortion.'

He wheeled away, his hands in his hair. 'Your husband didn't want you carrying someone else's child.'

'Strangely enough, no.'

'So you sacrificed your marriage for the sake of my child?'

She laughed, or attempted to at least before it became a hiccup instead and jerked her hands so that hot tea nearly sloshed over the top of her cup. She put it down on the bench beside her. 'I'm hardly that noble. I think my marriage was over a long time ago. I was just the last to know. He decided he might as well move in with his girlfriend when he learned it wasn't his baby I was carrying and when I refused to accept the clinic's offer to fix things.'

He just nodded, amazed at the inner strength of a woman he knew from experience could get blown over by a decent gust of wind, thankful for that inner strength, thankful for her circumstances. It suited him that the husband was gone. She would have no choice now.

He looked around the room, taking in the dated fittings and faded decor. The room was clean, he'd give her that much, but it was tired, as tired as this woman had looked when he'd met her today. 'So now you live here alone?'

She nodded.

'What about your family? Are they close?'

She shook her head. 'Mum died a few years back. I was an only child.'

'Your father?'

'I never knew him.'

Better and better. 'So who looks after you?'

'I look after me, Mr Pirelli,' she huffed, finding some of that lion-hearted feistiness she tapped into from time to time. 'I'm not a child.'

As much as he admired her courage, anger curled the corners of his senses. Her bastard husband had walked out on her. He'd abandoned her, leaving her pregnant and alone in a house in a suburb that only the brave-hearted or the criminal or those who couldn't afford to move out would choose.

She'd been alone since he'd gone. No wonder she looked so gaunt. Who was there to look after her? Who was there to ensure she ate properly or make sure she took proper care of herself? There was no other option.

'Get some things together,' he ordered. 'We're leaving.'

'What are you talking about?'

'You can't stay here. You're coming with me.'

'No, I'm not. This is my home. At least…' She trailed

off mid-sentence and Dominic found himself wondering how many more secrets she had left to reveal.

'At least what?'

'I got a letter today.' She nodded towards the table where the page still sat. Then she swallowed, her hands either side, gripping the bench top behind her. The action emphasized the leanness of her arms but, surprisingly, it also emphasized another part of her anatomy, one he hadn't taken much notice of until now. For, without her cardigan to cover her, her singlet top pulled tight across an anything-but-flat chest. What the hell was he thinking? He snatched up the letter, concentrated on that.

'Shayne took the car and most of the furniture when he left. He said that was enough. Now he's telling me he wants his share of the house. But it's my house! My mother left it to me. He can't do that, can he?'

The raw pain in her eyes touched him in a place he didn't know still existed. This house meant that much to her? But of course it would if it was all she had.

'I'll have my lawyers look into it,' he said, folding the letter. 'But you know you can't stay here. I don't want you staying here, knowing he's out there, knowing he could turn up at any time making demands.'

'I'm getting the locks changed.'

'You think that would stop him if he wanted to get in? No way in the world can I leave you here alone knowing he's out there, knowing what he wanted for my child. No way can I trust him anywhere near you. Don't you understand that?'

'But don't you still need his agreement to take this baby?'

'Let the lawyers take care of that as well. You think about what you need to pack just enough for tonight, I'll send my people to pick up the rest tomorrow.'

'Hang on. I haven't agreed to anything!'

'What do you have to stay for? You have no family and no husband. You have nothing, except a child that doesn't belong to you.'

How dared he talk to her like that—as if she was a nothing and a nobody he could order around at his whim? She stiffened her spine and kicked up her chin, sick of men who wanted to tell her what to do. 'I still have this house. Or at least a share of it.'

'And you're welcome to return to your share of it after the baby is born. Rest assured, I'll be the last person to stop you.'

She huffed off to her bedroom and packed her bag, just an overnight one for now, like he'd said, his words stinging in her ears as she flung in her pyjamas.

Damn the man!

So, maybe he had a point. Maybe she would be better off right away from here and from Shayne until this baby was born. Maybe it would be better for the baby. Safer.

She pulled open a drawer, grabbed some clean underwear and slammed it shut the way she would have liked to have slammed Mr Rule-The-World Pirelli with a few choice words of her own.

I'll be the last person to stop you. He'd said those words as if he couldn't wait to see the back of her.

Well, fine, she didn't want a baby and she sure didn't want to hang around him any longer than was absolutely necessary, but why had she been struck dumb? Why couldn't she have told him that?

I'll be the last person to stop you. Too late she thought of all the things she could have said—should have said—in response.

I wouldn't want you to stop me.

Just try to stop me.

You won't see me for dust.

But she'd said nothing and she knew why. Because his words had hurt. Because it hurt to feel so utterly worthless. It hurt to be abandoned. It hurt to know you were a loser and a failure on so many counts.

Hopeless wife.

Broken marriage.

She couldn't even manage to have the right baby.

Her underwear joined her pyjamas. She looked around the room. What else? He'd said he'd have his 'people' organise the removal of whatever else she needed tomorrow. Who the hell was this man that he had 'people' to do things, like a general with an entire army at his disposal, just waiting for him to bark out the next order?

She wrenched off her day-old top and pulled on a clean singlet top, threw another in the bag and reached for her thin cardigan, threading her arms through the sleeves. Too hot still for long sleeves but in the absence of full body armour she was going to need all the protection she could get.

The bathroom was her next stop, adding her hairbrush and a small bag of toiletries to her stash. She was back in the living room in ninety seconds flat.

He was making a call when she returned—probably organising a room for her somewhere or barking out more orders to his 'people', his eyebrows going north when he took her in. He snapped the phone shut. 'What took you so long?' he said as he reached for her bag and this time she almost did let fly with a few choice words. Until she saw the turned up lips and felt the urge to hit him instead. 'Cat got your tongue?'

'What's so funny?'

'You are. I thought the mouse was going to roar again.'

'What's that supposed to mean?'

'Doesn't matter.'

He took her bag and their hands brushed and she felt that unwanted sizzle of electricity again. His smile evaporated instantaneously.

'Don't do that!' she said.

'Do what?'

'Don't touch me.'

'My pleasure,' he said, his lips tight as he led her to his car, clearly unhappy to be lumbered with her. But that wasn't her problem.

Her problem was him.

She'd been furious. Blood-spitting furious. And then with one comment, one tiny tweak of his lips, she'd felt the rug pulled out from beneath her, leaving her senses reeling and her thought processes scrambled.

He'd smiled and she'd faltered and lost her train of thought along with her anger, even with that mouse reference? Was that how he thought of her? A mouse? Little, drab and ordinary. *And clearly amusing.* She bristled, not sure if she resented the fact he thought she was drab and amusing, even if she was to someone like him, more than the fact he seemed to occupy more than his fair share of the car. And what he didn't cover with his significant frame, his damn scent filled the rest.

Spicy and warm, woody and real.

Real.

There was that word again. She remembered she'd thought it the first time she'd seen him smile. Strange. She couldn't remember ever thinking it about any man before. Maybe it was because he was so unreal in so many ways. His obvious wealth. His mountain-like demeanour. The way he dominated a room or a restaurant or any other space just by being there. Maybe that was why she noticed it when he reminded her he was just a man.

Just a man?

Who was she trying to kid? He was unlike any man she'd ever met before. He had presence and power and the ability to set her skin alight with just the brush of his fingers. She shivered. He made her feel uncomfortable on so many levels and she didn't like it. She didn't want to feel so vulnerable and so aware of any man, married or not. After Shayne, she had sworn off men for ever.

Every last one of them. Especially the arrogant ones who wanted to rule her life. And especially the ones with black-as-night eyes who laughed at secret jokes at her expense.

Damn the man! She squirmed in her seat, the car filled with the scent of him, desperately needing a distraction.

'Where are you taking me?' she asked in the stony silence, when they had left the side streets of Sherwill far behind and were heading east along the ribbon of highway towards the city. The traffic was busier now, close to peak hour, the tailbacks longer.

'You'll see.'

'What if I don't like it?'

'You'll like it,' was all he offered, before he turned the radio on to the news channel, terminating the conversation. The stock market closing reports came on and Angie expected he'd change the channel, like Shayne had always done if he'd happened to stumble across it accidentally while flipping through the stations, but he didn't. He hung on every word. She tried to make sense of it but clearly they were speaking another language and she tuned out.

'What is it you actually do?' she asked when the report had finished and he'd turned the volume down again, the city closer now, the buildings in the distance ahead growing taller.

'The simple version? I invest.'

'What does that mean, exactly?'

'I play the share market. I buy shares low and sell them higher.'

She thought about it for a moment. 'So you don't actually make anything.'

'I make money and I use it to buy other things. Office blocks. Shopping centres.'

'I get it.' She wasn't sure why but the discussion seemed significant in getting a handle on how this man ticked. 'So you don't actually *produce* anything, then. Anything real, I mean. At the end of the day, what do you have to show for your efforts?'

'More money.'

Alongside him, she sighed, a strange little sigh of satisfaction, and he didn't like it. Not one bit. 'Do you have a problem with that?'

'Absolutely not.' She swept an appreciative hand along the designer dashboard, fiddled a bit with the buttons on the console. 'Clearly you must be awfully good at it.' He almost growled. He got the distinct impression her words had not been intended as a compliment.

His fingers tightened around the steering wheel. What was her problem? He'd dragged himself up from nothing. He'd turned himself into a billionaire, had half a dozen cars and a helicopter at his disposal and here she was saying he didn't make anything?

'I suppose you'd prefer it if I worked at a factory like your philandering husband.'

He caught the look in her eyes, shock giving way to a look of pain, as if she'd been deeply wounded, before she turned her head away.

And someone who wasn't used to apologising for anything or to anyone but who'd done their fair share lately suddenly felt like a heel again.

He might be ruthless in business, but that didn't mean he could go around kicking someone when she was down, even if she did provoke him. 'I'm sorry. I shouldn't have said that.'

'No. It's okay,' she said, now studying the hands knotted in her lap. 'I guess I asked for it. I'm sorry.'

'Do you miss him?'

Her head swung around—'Shayne?'—before setting into a shake. 'I think I actually miss the car more. The last few months have been... *difficult*. I guess if I'd had my eyes open, I might have seen it coming but the IVF treatment kind of takes your focus.'

Didn't he know it? 'There are always things we should have seen coming and yet somehow we miss them until it's too late.'

And he felt her cool blue eyes on him, felt their questions and their wondering. He kept his own eyes firmly fixed on the traffic.

In his peripheral vision he picked up her shrug. 'Anyway, I'm glad it's not Shayne's baby. I don't think I could have coped with learning about the affair while thinking I was carrying his child.'

Did she realise how wrong she was? This was a woman who'd been abandoned because she'd stood up to her husband and refused to abort a baby that wasn't even hers, a woman who was somehow planning to struggle through that pregnancy alone to give birth to a baby she didn't even plan on keeping. This was a woman who could pack an overnight bag in ninety seconds flat when most women he knew couldn't do it in under ninety minutes.

Sure, the woman might look like a mouse but she had a spine made of steel. It had taken courage to call him and even more courage to agree to meet him after that angry first phone call. And she'd been afraid—so afraid and so unsure and so quick to cower down as if she wished she could disappear. But, in spite of her fear, in spite of a sickness that left her weak and pale, she had turned up, only to have to defend herself against his accusations.

He glanced down at his watch before turning on the radio for another market update.

'Believe me,' he said gruffly, genuinely surprised to find a germ of respect for her in his thoughts, 'you would have coped.'

She didn't get a chance to ask him what he meant. He kept the radio on, absorbing a never ending stream of information. She tried to make sense of it. Minings. Industrials. NASDAQ. All Ords. But there was nothing she could relate to, nothing to anchor it to her life, and eventually she gave up and simply enjoyed the journey and the growing sense of anticipation welling up inside.

And she was excited, she realised. She'd left her home, the one home she could ever remember living in to go—where, exactly? He'd turned off one highway before reaching the city and onto another major road that seemed to snake its way though tree-lined suburbs that looked more and more wealthy, the houses bigger, the gardens more and more beautiful. Every now and then she'd get a glimpse of harbour and blue water and anticipation bubbled up inside. It was like going on one of those mystery holidays where you didn't know where you were going until you got to the airport, not that she ever had. But Shayne had used to talk about doing one some time. He might actually do it now with Abigail.

No! She gave herself a mental slap to the head. She refused to waste her time thinking about Shayne. Not now. Not after all the things he'd done. Wherever she was going, it would be much better than anything she could do with Shayne. Dominic Pirelli might be arrogant and controlling and judgemental, but he wasn't cheap.

Wherever he had in mind for her accommodation for the next however many months, it wouldn't be substandard. Maybe not because he cared about her, but because he wanted the best for his baby.

Which wouldn't be so very hard to take, really. It would be like having a holiday at someone else's expense.

A six-month holiday.

Why shouldn't she at least try to enjoy it?

The snatches of sea became more frequent and the concept of a holiday more tantalizing and seductive by the minute. They were close to the beach now. She could smell the tang of salt in the air—such a different air to where she'd come from, where the air seemed weighted down with dust and heat and desperation. And then he pulled into a street filled with houses that looked like mansions where the sea lapped practically at their feet.

And, not for the first time today, anticipation changed direction and changed into a spinning ball of nerves. Surely not anywhere this grand? And then he slowed to enter a driveway blocked by a massive set of gates that must have stood at least ten feet tall in order to match the whitewashed walls either side.

'This is it,' he said. He turned off the radio and hit a button somewhere and the gates swung slowly open, her jaw also automatically swinging open, though much quicker than the gates.

This wasn't a house, she could tell as he drove inside and the full splendour of the home was revealed. At least two levels. Probably three, all facing out to sea with what looked like a pool she could glimpse behind a bougainvillea-covered fence and with the sea lapping the rock-strewn shore below.

Definitely not a mere house. It was a mansion. Where was the unit or apartment she'd half expected—the place where he could easily keep an eye on her and monitor his baby's progress—without her getting in anyone's way?

'But surely this is your home.'

'It is.' He cast an eye down to her belly. 'And that's my child. Where else should it be?'

She swallowed, thinking she might as well have shifted planets rather than suburbs, because to live here, in a place like this, was beyond her wildest imaginings. It was beyond...anything. But when she'd contemplated having this couple's child, she'd always imagined remaining at arm's length. She would have the baby and hand it over to its rightful parents after it was born. The last thing she'd expected was to move in with them for the duration. It wasn't as if she was family, after all...

He opened her door for her and retrieved her bag from the back seat and still she hadn't moved, but what else was new? Ever since that phone call she'd made yesterday—was it only yesterday?—things had been happening too fast for her to keep up.

'Are you coming?' Impatience threaded through his words and she realised he'd spent his entire afternoon chasing after her. No doubt he couldn't wait to be rid of her and get back to making his millions. She'd probably cost him a fortune already.

'Look,' she said, unclicking her seat belt and stepping out reluctantly, but only so he didn't appear so large beside her and so she didn't appear like some recalcitrant child throwing a tantrum. What she really needed most was her own space, somewhere she felt comfortable— even if it was only a hovel compared to this palace—not to live cheek by jowl with the parents of her child. But refusing to come out of the car was hardly any way to convince him.

'I don't want to appear ungrateful, but I'm not convinced this is a good idea. I mean, how's it going to look to everyone if you move some random pregnant woman into your family home? People are going to talk. I really think it would be better for everyone if I went somewhere else.'

He stiffened alongside her, the man becoming mountain again, his eyes darkly intense, his jaw as stiff as if it had been chiselled from stone. 'There's something you obviously don't understand about me, Mrs Cameron. I don't actually give a damn how things look or what people say or think.'

Least of all her. She knew for a fact he didn't give a damn what she thought. But that didn't mean she'd stop trying to make him see sense. 'I realise you have little reason to care about my needs and wants—you have different priorities—but have you thought for one moment about what your wife might think of this plan? Surely you must realise this arrangement will make things awkward for her?'

He took a deep breath and looked skywards, running one hand through his dark hair before he whipped off his sunglasses and rubbed his eyes with the back of the other. With the sun on his face, she could make out the strain lines etched around his eyes and the sudden tight line of his mouth. 'I assumed you would have known,' he said, his deep voice coarse like a dry riverbed. 'It's not exactly a secret, after all.'

'Known what?' she asked, confused, her mind clicking over before seizing on the obvious answer—an answer she should have considered before now, given her own pathetic circumstances. But why should hers be the only marriage to fail? She cursed herself for never considering that very real possibility but instead choosing to believe some kind of fairy tale ending for the child with a mother and a father who both wanted it and would both cherish and love it together. And now she didn't know if the mother even knew about the baby's existence. Or was the father, by bringing her to his place, making a de facto claim for custody?

It was all going so wrong! She should have insisted on meeting the mother. She should never have let her fantasies get in the way of reality. She sighed. 'You're telling me you're divorced?'

'Not divorced!' His words ground their way through the morass of her mind. 'My wife is dead.'

CHAPTER SIX

His wife was dead? The mother of the baby she was carrying was dead?

Angie was stunned. Sickened beyond belief.

Poor baby, she thought, the palm of one hand instinctively going to her belly. Poor, poor baby to grow up with no mother.

And then right on the heels of that thought, poor Dominic. His wife was dead and then some stranger turns up on his doorstep pregnant with their child. No wonder he'd been so angry when she'd called! No wonder he'd been so quick to judge—so openly resentful—denied his own wife, only for Angie to turn up claiming to be carrying their baby.

Tears pricked her eyes. Tears of sadness. Tears of loss. Tears for a baby that would be born in circumstances surrounded by so much tragedy. It was as if the weight of the world was pressing down on the shoulders of this child and it wasn't even born.

And she'd been so wrong. All the while she'd imagined he was protecting his wife by not bringing her to their meeting! She'd half resented him for wanting to check her out first, knowing he'd found her wanting, even wondering if he'd even bothered to tell his wife. But how was he supposed to tell his wife? How could he?

Oh, God, what a mess!

She looked up at him now, at this dark mountain of a man, his eyes black with resentment for her, his hands curled into fists by his sides and she wanted to weep for him, weep at the unfairness that had resulted in her being the one to bear his child, weep for the trauma instead of the joy that should have accompanied this child's existence.

The sting of tears became too much and moisture soon dewed her eyes and spilled over onto her cheeks. She'd been so quick to judge him without knowing all the facts.

'I'm so sorry,' she said, reaching out a hand to his arm.

'No!' He yanked his arm away before she'd barely brushed it with her fingertips. 'I don't want your pity!'

She reeled away. She should have known he'd take anything she said the wrong way. She seemed to bring out the worst in him. She seemed unable to stop herself. 'What would you prefer me to admit? That I'm actually relieved to learn you're not making some kind of under-handed custody bid by locking me away here?'

His eyes narrowed, lit by the kind of heat that had nothing to do with the sun and everything to do with raw anger. 'You think me capable of that?'

She swallowed, blue eyes meeting black. 'It did cross my mind.'

'You think so little of me, I'm surprised you would even trust me with my own child. Does it gall you now to go through with this?'

She turned her head away. 'That's not up to me.'

'No, it's not. But still you judge. You think I care more for money than I do for this child. I fall short of expectations because I don't make nuts and bolts. Instead, I make money, which is what every damn person making nuts and bolts is trying to make. And yet somehow my success lowers me in your eyes.'

She shook her head. 'And you don't think you judge me? You haven't stopped judging me since the moment we met. Judging me and damning me and now locking me away in some gilded bloody cage.'

'It's hardly a cage!'

'And you don't consider my feelings. I'm not sure I should stay here. Not under the circumstances. Not with your wife gone. It doesn't feel right.'

'What?' He slammed one hand down on the car roof alongside her, sending her skywards. 'First you didn't want to stay here because my wife might object. Now you won't stay because she can't. What are you really worried about, Mrs Cameron—that I might try to jump your skinny bones while you're under my roof?'

'No!' Her face was burning up with indignation. Burning up with the stinging barb contained within his words. Jump her skinny bones? No way in the world. 'You think I'd let you if you tried?'

'Or that after a taste of the high life, you won't want to go home?' His skin was drawn tight, tendons cording in his neck while a savage pulse beat at his temple.

'Fat chance. A person would have to be some kind of masochist to want to stay with you. I promise you, if I stay—and that's a big if—it's only until this child is born, and then you won't see me for dust.'

'Good.' He sniffed and pushed himself away from the car. 'So we understand each other perfectly, then. You have my assurance I won't be tempted to take advantage of you and I have your assurance we're not going to have separation issues in six months' time. Seems we have the perfect arrangement.'

Perfect arrangement?

Or perfect hell?

And suddenly six months under the same roof with this man didn't sound like any sort of holiday at all. And still they remained there, glaring at each other, and there was no way she was going to break eye contact first lest he took that as some sort of victory.

'Dominic, you're here.' The quietly spoken voice came from behind. He broke eye contact first and Angie rubbed her arms, grateful for the interruption. She turned to see an older woman, slim and smartly dressed. She smiled. 'And you must be Angelina Cameron. Such a pretty name,' the woman said, taking both her hands in her own, her smile wide though her eyes looked troubled as they flicked from one arrival to the other. 'Come in, dear. I've been expecting you.'

'Angelina, this is Rosa, my housekeeper,' said Dominic coarsely, performing the formalities. 'Although, as you will no doubt learn, she is much more than a mere housekeeper.'

Rosa's smile widened at that, her eyes creasing with love that still held more than a hint of concern. Angie followed stiffly as Rosa led them along a covered walkway leading to the house, wondering how long it was since she'd been called by her full name. Probably the last time she'd renewed her driver's licence. She decided she liked Rosa. Her welcome had been genuine, her warm hands squeezing hers almost as if saying *I understand*. She liked the way her name had sounded on Dominic's lips even more. What was it about the way his deep voice could sound her name?

Rosa glanced over her shoulder, smiling as she caught Angie's eyes. What had Dominic told her? Did she know why she was here? Or was she merely in the habit of welcoming Dominic's women? She didn't know the circumstances of his wife's death or how long ago it had occurred, but she couldn't imagine a man like him staying single for long.

It simply wasn't possible. He was much too good-looking. Entirely too masculine. Power radiated from him, almost a tangible thing, or was that just his heat she could feel as he walked at her shoulder? She glanced back, pretending to take in the view. No, she thought. Not just heat, but power oozed from him.

With all he had going for him—his looks, his wealth, his beautiful home—he no doubt had women lining up to become the next Mrs Pirelli. With a small baby to look after, he'd be utterly irresistible.

If you were into the kind of man who judged a woman by her looks and where she came from.

And then Rosa led them beyond the manicured gardens and into the house proper and Angie momentarily forgot about the man beside her. For if the outside of the house was palatial, the inside beggared belief. To the right of the entrance hallway one massive room ran along the length of the house, arched windows over the French windows leading onto a terrace overlooking the sea with glittering chandeliers hanging from the impossibly high ceiling. She gaped. This was like something from a fairy tale. Cinderella had probably danced here.

'I've prepared the guest suite for you,' Rosa said, jerking her attention back. 'I hope you'll be comfortable there.'

Angie couldn't respond. She was still having trouble believing this palace was someone's home. Maybe even hers for the next six months.

Her suite turned out to be in its own wing. Rosa beamed as she led the way into rooms decorated in tones of lemon and white with blue accents. Late afternoon sunshine slanted through curtains fluttering in the sea breeze. It was too much for Angie to take in. Beyond the sitting room there was a massive bedroom, the bed a king-sized masterpiece with its own dressing room and a window that looked out over the cliffs and the sea. The en suite bathroom beyond was unbelievably decadent in white marble with a sunken spa and double-sized shower.

For something referred to casually as a suite, she realised, it was bigger than her entire house in Sherwill. And one hell of a lot more luxurious.

'Will it do?' Dominic asked after the tour had concluded, depositing her bag on the blanket box at the end of the bed. 'Do you think you'll be comfortable here?' And for the first time she sensed a hint of insecurity. Was he so worried she'd take his baby away? But his *Will it do?*—who was he trying to kid?

'You've seen where I come from. What do you think?'

'Then I'll take that as a yes,' he said. 'I have work to catch up on. The rest of your things will be here tomorrow. Let Rosa know if you need anything else in the meantime and she'll take care of it. I'll see you at dinner.'

'Thank you. I appreciate it,' she said, meaning every word, looking around at the plush fittings and decor and secretly relishing the idea of this suite being hers for the next six months. Hardly some kind of jail sentence. Unless she thought about who she was being locked up with. Thank God he had an office to go to. With any luck, he'd work long hours and she'd never see him.

And then she sensed movement and turned and found

he'd gone, with just a hint of his tantalising woody masculine scent remaining on the air.

Across the room, Rosa smiled softly at her. 'It is good you are here,' she said. 'For too long he has been alone. And now to have a baby...' she put her hands over her mouth but Angie had already seen the tremors even as she'd pressed her lips together, had already seen the moisture sheening her eyes '...a baby is like a gift from the heavens. You must be a very special woman, to do this thing for Dominic.'

And Angie felt her own tears well up again, shaking her head in a futile effort to make them go away. She wasn't special or noble or unselfish. Her reasons were far more personal. 'It had nothing to do with Dominic,' she insisted. 'I'm just pleased this baby has found its home. A place where it is wanted.'

The light glinted off Rosa's tear-laden eyes as she nodded, blinking and blotting her cheeks dry with a handkerchief. 'And I am forgetting myself. What would you like? Can I get you something to eat, or perhaps I could run you a bath? It will relax you. Or maybe you'd like a swim in the pool?'

So many choices and all of them so inviting! But she wasn't hungry yet after that huge lunch and she hadn't packed bathers. She looked longingly in the direction of the bathroom. That marble-tiled, gold-tapped submerged bath looked like temptation itself. So much decadence should be illegal or at the very least immoral, but the concept of submerging herself within its watery depths was like a lure to the senses. 'The bath sounds wonderful.'

Rosa nodded, pulling a white plush robe from the wardrobe and laying it on the bed. 'I'll run it for you and then bring you a cup of tea. We have ginger and green tea, unless you'd prefer something else?'

'That would be perfect,' Angie said, thanking her, wondering what guardian angel had deposited her here, into Rosa's warm and welcoming care. Not Dominic, she knew. He might want to guard her for the next six months, but if he was an angel, he was definitely of the dark variety, complex and—she searched for a word to describe him—*dangerous*.

It fitted, she thought, trembling just a little as she changed into the robe. Definitely dangerous. Maybe not physically threatening, in spite of his size and presence. More the kind of danger that operated on another level.

For his danger came in dark eyes that could unnerve and unsettle, look at her with undisguised disdain or, in the very next look, send heat spiralling through her. His danger was that dark longing that left her weak and breathless.

And when he touched her...

She shivered. Forget about Dominic and guardian angels and touching, she told herself, the perfumed steam coming from the bathroom beckoning with the scent of rosemary and orange and maybe even a hint of vanilla. Maybe, for just once in her life, something was going right. Maybe these next six months would be the perfect opportunity to work out what she wanted to do with the rest of her life.

After all, she was single now. No ties. She could make a fresh start. Maybe do some study? Make something of herself.

And as for this baby? She curled a hand over her tummy, her heart aching for the mother who would never know her child, and for the child who would never know its mother. She'd so wanted everything to be perfect for this baby! But still she'd made the right choice, she knew. This baby would have a home. The baby was wanted. What more could she really ask?

She put a toe in the bath and sighed, slipping off her robe as she slid into the depths and adjusting the spa jets to a slow pulsing massage that sent tremors under her skin, tremors that triggered her senses and echoed another's electric touch, a watery assault to her senses that had her almost imagining the touch of his fingers, the slide of his hands...

She snapped her eyes open, hit the button that turned the spa jets off, appalled at where her thoughts were taking her.

No! For he was the biological father of the child she was carrying, the husband of the biological mother who was dead. A man who detested her for who and what she was.

What the hell was wrong with her?

She dunked her head under the water to clear her wayward thoughts. No way would she fantasize about him!

An hour later, wrapped in the fluffy robe, Angie felt blissfully relaxed as she padded through the house, looking for the kitchen, every bone and muscle in her body purring after the scented soaking, so relaxed that not even the cup and saucer rattled in her hand. She'd imagined the kitchen wouldn't be hard to find but then she'd forgotten the sheer scale of the place. On their way to the suite she'd only encountered passages and hallways and that amazing sweep of ballroom lining the front of the house. But surely the kitchen couldn't be too far away?

She paused in a wide hallway she was suddenly sure she'd never passed before because of the wide staircase leading upwards to another floor, and turned full circle, wondering where she'd taken a wrong turn. How big was this place that she could get lost within its walls?

And then she glanced upstairs and saw it.

The portrait stretched along the landing wall—a painting of a woman reclining along an ivory chaise longue, her long hair dark and sleek and tumbling over satin-skinned shoulders, her face beautiful, dark exotic eyes enticing, carmine lips turned up in invitation, her body draped in a gown the colour of deepest amethyst.

The face and body of a seductress.

Angie climbed up a step. And then another.

She was beautiful.

And realisation came dressed in a sharp, short stab of envy. This was Carla. This was the real mother of her unborn child.

Was it any surprise Dominic had been so appalled when he'd met her? Was it any surprise he'd been angry? This glamorous creature was the woman supposed to be carrying their child, not some scarecrow from the wrong end of town.

She jumped as a door snicked shut somewhere close and then Dominic appeared on the landing, stopping when he saw her halfway up the stairs, his dark eyes fixing her. 'Angelina?'

Angie couldn't move, held captive by those damning eyes. Would he think she'd been snooping? Would he take her for a thief? He already thought the worst of her; it would only be a small jump to make. The cup rattled against the saucer in her hand. She put the other one out to steady it. 'I'm sorry. I was actually looking for the kitchen to return my cup. I must have taken the wrong turn.'

His eyes flicked down to the cup in her hand and back to her face as if he was measuring her words and weighing them for truth. He started down the stairs towards her, his long legs carrying him down, step by decisive step. He'd changed from his business clothes into dark trousers and a slim-fitting T-shirt, the fabric so fine it seemed to skim over the wall of his chest and accentuate his perfect proportions. He stopped on the step alongside her and she saw the tiny beads of water clinging to his hair, smelt his recently showered masculine freshness. She tugged the edges of her robe together, suddenly conscious of the fabric against her nipples, feeling hopelessly unprepared for another meeting with this man. 'The kitchen is not upstairs.'

She swallowed. 'I know. I'm sorry. I saw the portrait. Is that... Is that your wife?' She looked back at the portrait, feeling a bone-deep ache she didn't care to analyse too much. The dark beauty was perfect for him. Polished and elegant and unerringly confident with it.

'That's Carla, yes.'

'She was so beautiful.'

Dominic glanced back over his shoulder at the portrait. 'She was.' Then he took a deep breath and started down the rest of the steps. 'Follow me. I'll show you how to find the kitchen.'

He disappeared after he'd handed her into Rosa's care in the massive kitchen, his car keys in his hand, telling Rosa he'd be back late. Angie wondered if he had a date as she watched him leave. She would be beautiful, of course. She'd have to be to attract a man like him, a man used to being surrounded by beautiful things...

'Do you like tortellini?'

Angie blinked, Rosa's question grounding her. 'I don't know. I've never had it.' And Rosa just smiled as she put the plate in front of her.

Angie discovered she loved it. Especially home-made, as she learned Rosa's was. 'Did Mr Pirelli put you up to this?' she asked, polishing off her second helping as she pushed wet hair she wished she'd dried out of her eyes. 'Did he tell you I needed filling out? He thinks I'm too skinny.'

Rosa just laughed. 'I'm Italian too, *cara*. To me, everyone needs filling out. And you especially must keep up your strength. You are doing a very important job. Some would say the most important job in the world.'

Angie put down her fork and thanked her, feeling deliciously full for the second time today, still thinking about that portrait and the woman who should be carrying this child. 'I saw Carla's…Mrs Pirelli's…portrait on the landing. She was beautiful.'

The older woman gave a sad smile as she took Angie's plate. 'That was painted shortly after they were married. She was a beautiful girl. She wanted desperately for a child to give Dominic. In the end… Well, in the end it just didn't happen.'

Angie's hand curled over her belly. 'It's not fair that she's not here for this. It's not fair that I've got her baby.'

And Rosa put a reassuring hand to her shoulder. 'It's a miracle, that's what it is.' She looked down at Angie's empty plate and smiled though Angie sensed her sadness in the moisture that glossed her eyes. 'Truly it is a miracle.' Then she huffed in a breath, gathering herself as she carried it to the sink. 'Well, what would you like to do now? Do you need anything I can help you with while you settle in?'

Angie shook her head. 'It's been a long day. I might turn in early.' Although, she thought as she pushed her fringe out of her eyes again, there was one thing she could tackle. 'You don't have some scissors I could borrow, do you? My hair is driving me crazy.'

Rosa nodded decisively as if she had the perfect solution. 'I have a better idea. I have a niece who is a hairdresser. She works from home. I will call her, see if she can't drop by tomorrow morning.'

'There's no need—'

But Rosa just held up her hand as she reached for the phone, the matter apparently decided.

That night Angie lay in an unfamiliar bed, listening to unfamiliar sounds—the swoosh of waves on the rock-strewn shore below, the call of seabirds, the scamper of tiny marsupials through the tree tops. All so very different. All so very strange. She snuggled deeper into the cloud-soft bed. How would she ever sleep?

She stirred to the soft billow of curtain and a fresh sea breeze, the scent of hot tea and toast coming from the bedside table, blinking into wakefulness when she saw it was after ten. She hadn't slept that long in for ever. She eased herself up and took a sip of tea, testing her stomach, then cautiously nibbled at some toast. A little queasy but much better than yesterday. She took her time, not rushing herself. Maybe the doctor was right. Maybe she would get past this horrid stage. She could only hope.

An hour later Rosa's niece arrived. She was on leave now, she explained, while her *bambinos* were small. Right now, Rosa entertained her *bambinos* with cheese straws and building blocks in one corner of the kitchen while Antonia studied Angie's face and ran her fingers through her hair. 'You have a natural wave, you know,' she said, nodding as she poked and prodded. 'But the weight drags it down. I've got an idea what we can do. Are you game?'

An hour of snipping, a deep condition and blow-dry later, Angie looked in the mirror and couldn't believe the transformation. This was her hair? Where once it had hung lank and lifeless around her face, or been pulled back into a tight ponytail, now her hair bounced and flicked in layers around her face.

'I love it!' she announced, to the delight of Antonia and Rosa. 'How can I ever repay you?'

Rosa smiled and hugged her niece. 'Believe me. You already have.'

She looked—different. He couldn't quite pinpoint the change as they sat at the dining table that evening. She was still wearing what looked like the same jeans and another of those singlet tops she seemed to have an endless supply of, the same dreary cardigan pulled over the top, but her eyes looked bigger in her face, her mouth somehow wider.

And every now and then he'd catch a hint of something—her perfume? Whatever, it was fresh and fascinating, with a hint of fruit he could almost identify. Almost pin down. And then Rosa would bring in another dish and he would lose sight of it again.

'How are you settling in?' he asked, trying to make small talk. He was used to eating alone, usually in his office as he kept an eye on the overseas markets, but tonight he had papers for her that needed signing. Besides, he supposed he should at least be civil. She was, after all, a guest in his house. He reached for the still steaming basket of bread, only to inadvertently touch her hand as she reached for the same slice.

He pulled it back while hers disappeared into her lap. He flexed his fingers and this time claimed his bread, musing. He didn't know if she was charged with static electricity because her clothes were full of artificial fibres, but every time he touched her she seemed to spark under his skin.

'Everything's fine,' she answered blandly, yet the colour in her cheeks belied her tone, her voice carrying a noticeable quake.

'I have some paperwork from the lawyers for you to sign after dinner if you're up to it.'

She perked up immediately. 'Do you have news about the house?'

He shook his head, saw the hope in her eyes die and wondered if he should share the news. Decided she had a right to know the truth. 'But the lawyers say he's entitled to make a claim, even though the property was in your name.' Why she was so obsessed with the old place was beyond him, though he could understand why she thought it was unfair Shayne should get anything of hers after the way he'd treated her. 'The lawyers are still looking into it. This is actually about our agreement.'

She looked at him blankly, as if her mind was still worrying about the house she might lose.

'You don't have to do it today if you want to check it with another lawyer. There's no rush.' And then he sat there wondering why he'd just said that. He wanted everything in writing as soon as possible. He didn't want any chance of her changing her mind or developing a taste for the high life and demanding more. He wanted this thing nailed down now.

'It's okay,' she said numbly. 'Best to know where everyone stands from the start.' She nodded then and he was suddenly transfixed by the movement in her hair.

That was what was so different. There were layers of it, he realised, and as she moved her head they shifted, independently and yet together, like a field of wheat rippling in the breeze, with feathery ends flicking playfully in the light.

And then he focused again and she was watching him, wary and unsure. 'I might actually skip dessert and get an early night,' she said. 'Maybe if I could just sign those documents now?'

'It's too much!' she protested ten minutes later in his office. 'Nobody needs twenty thousand dollars a month for living expenses.'

'How do you know?' he argued back, wishing she'd just sign it if she was in such a goddamn hurry to get back to her suite and trying to ignore the way the layers of her hair bobbed around her head as she moved and the scent of raspberries and oranges that seemed to be taking over his office. 'You'll need new clothes as the baby grows. Let's face it, you could do with some new clothes now.'

Her cheeks flamed with heat. 'But twenty thousand dollars? You clearly don't know where I shop.'

'So shop somewhere else. Or save the money! Book a cruise. Give it to charity. I don't care what you do with it—just sign the agreement.'

If she could tell he sounded tense he didn't care. He wanted her out of his office. She was too close, that damned scent of fruit wrapping around him, the soft layers of her hair dancing an invitation with even the slightest tilt of her head. And what it did to her eyes! She had the most amazing eyes. Not just blue. On a paint chart they'd probably call it 'cerulean dreaming'.

He backed away, ostensibly to give her more room

at the desk but in reality to give himself a chance to get his head together.

What was happening to him? His office had seemed a good choice a few minutes ago. Businesslike and masculine, he'd reasoned, how he liked his office to be. But somehow right now with this woman looking over a document on his desk, he was having trouble remembering what businesslike felt like. He had no such trouble when it came to remembering masculine.

His hormones were clearly dusty if he was feeling attracted to this woman.

'All right,' she conceded tightly. 'It's your money, after all,' and he blew out a long breath he hadn't realised he'd been holding as finally she signed her name first on one copy and then the other. 'Where else did you say to initial?' she asked, and he was forced to move closer again, flicking a page in the document she was looking at and pointing to where she needed to put her mark. But it was her hair his eyes were drawn to as he leaned over her, and how the ends danced and flirted with his every breath, as if they were alive and oh, so responsive.

She turned her head then, her face perilously close to his, her blue eyes wide with surprise, her lips parted on a question, and right at that moment he thought that whatever her question was, he was the answer.

'Mr Pirelli?' she breathed, and he drank her in.

'Dominic,' he corrected, his eyes not leaving lips that looked surprisingly like an invitation. Why had he not noticed that before?

'Dominic…'

He loved the way his name looked on her lips; he liked the neat white line of teeth below and the hint of pink tongue.

And then his mobile phone rang in his pocket and the

spell was broken. He wheeled away, appalled, wondering what the hell he'd been thinking.

Angie scrawled her initials on the papers, hopefully somewhere near the place he'd indicated, and made for the door. She needed to get outside and breathe, for there was no air left in the room, no life-sustaining oxygen to be had. Somehow it had all burnt up in one smouldering look from his dark eyes. But they hadn't just been dark tonight. They'd been black.

She stumbled from the room, her heart racing as she headed for the kitchen, nearly bumping into Rosa on her way out. 'Oh. I was just coming to see if you both wanted dessert now, or at least a warm drink.'

'Nothing for me,' Angie managed, knowing her cheeks were aflame with colour. 'I think I'll go straight to bed. Goodnight.'

'I just think you should have got her an apartment some-where,' Simone protested down the line. 'Are you sure it was such a good idea to move her into your place?'

'I couldn't let her stay out there where she was!'

'Well, no. But to have her move in with you? Look, Dom, you should be careful with someone like her. Next thing you know, she'll get used to luxury living and you'll never get rid of her.'

'We have an agreement. She signed it tonight. She leaves as soon as the baby is delivered.'

'And you really believe she'll go back to where she came from, after seeing how the other half lives?'

'Why, Simone,' he said, half joking, 'anyone would think you cared.'

A moment's hesitation. 'I just don't want anyone taking advantage of you, that's all.'

He remembered the almost kiss in the study—tried

to work out if it was Angie who'd precipitated what had almost happened or him—and gave up trying. In the end nothing had happened and that was how it would stay. 'Forget it, Simone. You know me. You really think that after so many years of business I'd let someone like her take advantage of me?'

There was an uncomfortable silence on the other end of the line. 'She's a woman, Dominic. And, if you haven't noticed, she's carrying your child, and now we learn her husband's dumped her. Of course she's going to play on your heart strings every chance she gets. Arrangement or not, what has she got to lose by trying?'

'Thanks for the warning,' he said. 'Not that I think there's too much chance of me falling for someone like her, do you?'

At the end of the phone line Simone laughed, exactly the reaction he'd intended, but as he terminated the call a few moments later he told himself that he'd only spoken the truth. There was no chance in the world he'd be taken in by someone like Angie Cameron. Sure, maybe he thought her new haircut suited her, but he hadn't actually kissed her, had he? Nothing had happened. Nothing would happen. He'd make sure of it. He'd stay out of her way. Take dinner in his office as if nothing had changed.

Because nothing really had changed. It wasn't as if she was an invited guest. They had a contract, one that said nothing about him having to entertain her for the duration. Once she fulfilled the terms, she'd leave.

After all, surely he hadn't come this far to start slumming it now.

CHAPTER SEVEN

TONIGHT sleep eluded her, despite the smooth white sheets and fluffy comforter and the crash of waves on the rocks below.

What had she been thinking in his office? He'd seemed tense. Nervy even, as if she was cramping his style. And so she'd decided to sign the damn contract so she could get out of there, except she'd sensed something fanning her hair and turned suddenly, and he'd been right there behind her—*right there*! And the way he'd looked at her, with those dark eyes heated and intense, she'd felt that tug, that insane longing once again.

She should have turned right back around. She should have stood up and told him she'd need to read the agreement over again in her suite, but she'd stayed there for a moment too long, and then he'd leaned towards her and she'd waited. Waited for what?

For him to kiss her?

She rolled over and dragged a pillow over her head. Oh, God she was crazy! Pregnancy hormones were making her crazy. And just why would billionaire Dominic Pirelli try to kiss her? He, no doubt, had the pick of Sydney society to entertain if he so wished.

He was nothing to her. Nothing but the biological father of the baby she happened to be carrying in her womb.

And she was nothing to him.

Less than nothing; he'd made that patently clear. So what was she thinking, that she even imagined he'd wanted to kiss her?

Crazy!

But there would be no more chance of crazy moments like that. Her suite was self-contained. She would plead tiredness and take her evening meals alone. And save them all some embarrassment and angst in the process.

The waves crashed in against the shore, water whooshing up the sandy cove before silence reigned for a few seconds and there was another crash, another whoosh.

She loved the sounds here, loved the sound of the sea so close. She heard a bird cry in the darkness, a seabird settling down, embracing the night.

Sounds so different from what she was used to. A difference she was determined not to grow accustomed to.

Not if she could help it.

The garage lights came on with a sudden snap and settled into a low hum. Usually his office was his retreat. Normally he could bury himself there for hours. But not tonight, not with the hint of fruit still on the air and the memories of a girl with brilliant blue eyes and lips he'd come too close to kissing. Tonight his office was no sanctuary at all.

Dominic cast his eyes around the long room, more like a car park than any mere garage. His half dozen favourite vehicles sat gleaming under the lights, ready for action, and as he looked around the room, his gaze lingered wistfully over the red Ferrari. It had been some time since he'd taken that baby out for a run and right now he could do with it more than ever.

But he turned away, his gaze going to the workshop beyond the cavernous showroom, because he wasn't here to check out his collection of cars. It had been years since he'd last seen what he was looking for, but he'd kept them, he knew, so they had to be down here somewhere.

It took him an hour of searching but eventually he found them, buried deep in the shelving that lined the wall above the workbench. And what had first looked like nothing more than an old bundle of cloth was unrolled to reveal its treasure. His poppa's woodworking tools—the gouges and chisels his grandfather had used to carve the tiny birds and animals that had adorned their home and the ornate carvings, the crucifixes and benevolent-eyed Madonnas he had sold to make a little extra money.

The wooden handles seemed darker than he remembered, stained with time and neglect, though the steels still looked keen edged and true. Just looking at them took him back to another era, another time. He lifted a gouge, testing it in his palm, never expecting it to feel so right—his poppa's hands had always seemed so big compared to his—only to find the weight sat perfectly. His fingers curled around the wooden handle, settling into the long ago worn grooves from another's hand.

He bowed his head, his eyes squeezed shut as the memories surged back. Powerful. Overwhelming. Of sitting on his poppa's knee at the long workbench in the shed out back while his big hands guided his own, showing him how to work the gouge with the grain to shape the wood, and then to give detail with the different chisels. He'd shown him how to smooth the surface and then he'd learned how to polish with the slipstones until the surface was slick to the touch.

He'd wrapped the piece in cotton wool and a scrap of used birthday wrapping. Nonna had found a red ribbon to tie around it and he'd given it to his mother for her birthday.

The best present she'd ever had, she'd told him, and his poppa had beamed while his heart had swelled with pride.

When had he forgotten how to make things?

Right about the time he'd learned how important it was to have money.

Right about the time he'd learned that without money you were powerless to save the ones you loved.

But it hadn't saved Carla.

Angry, he headed for the bin of offcuts the last lot of builders had left behind after they'd finished the gazebo by the pool. He fossicked for a bit before pulling out a piece six inches long. It wasn't hardwood. His grandfather wouldn't approve. But it would do.

He sat at the bench surveying the piece of wood, his fingers curling and flexing over the tools all lined up in their now flattened leather roll. He picked up the wood in one hand and a gouge in the other and attacked a corner. The tool skidded away, never gaining purchase, almost taking off a fingertip. He cursed, sharp and sweet, hearing his poppa's voice in his ear advising him, imagined his old worn hand guiding his own.

He took a deep breath, angled the tool and tried again.

He sat back and took a deep breath. Sweat rolled off him as if he'd just run ten kilometres along the shore. He glanced at his watch, astonished to find two hours had passed since he'd sat down and started curling wood shavings from the block, totally focused as he searched for the object that lay within. It had felt good to hold the tools. Good to feel their power and their potential.

He'd even imagined he was getting somewhere.

He looked critically down at the piece in his hands now, turning it one way and then the other before he hurled the lump back into the bin where it landed with a clatter.

It was rubbish!

She was bored. Beyond bored. Angie put down her book, even that failing to hold her interest. One month of having nothing to do but eat, sleep or swim laps of the pool and Angie was fast running out of enthusiasm for her six-month holiday. Even the fact she was feeling better, her morning sickness easing, was no consolation. At least throwing up half the day had given her something to do.

Inspired both by Dominic's insult about her wardrobe and the sad truth of the state of the clothes that had been delivered with her belongings, she'd asked Rosa to see if Antonia would mind coming shopping with her.

It turned out Antonia had been just the person for the job. Angie had drawn the line at the ball gowns— the way her tummy was finally starting to show, they wouldn't fit her ten minutes after she'd bought them, and where would she wear them anyway, but she'd still managed to come home with an entire wardrobe of clothes and shoes and with a new appreciation for how far twenty thousand dollars didn't go when you lived on this side of town.

She loved her new clothes. She loved the way the bright sundresses made her feel—feminine and pretty.

She loved the cool linen trousers and soft tops and sandals she'd bought to go with them. She loved the flirty floral skirts that shifted on the breeze as she walked.

She loved her new look, even with the way her waist was thickening, her body changing. She was putting on weight and she liked it and insanely she wanted Dominic to notice, to see that she didn't always look like something the cat had dragged in. But he never seemed to be around, instead always busy or buried away in his office or the garage downstairs. And as much as she loved Rosa, it would be nice to talk to another adult every now and then.

She sighed. Right now she was all shopped out, swimming pooled out and relaxed out. Even sitting reading in her favourite spot in the ballroom with the ocean just outside was beginning to lose its appeal. She needed to do something.

She headed for the kitchen, with its granite-topped benches and white cupboard doors and hanging pots and pans, and where Rosa took pity on her and sent her out to get milk. She came back from the local supermarket a few minutes later with the milk, an application form and a smile a mile wide.

'What are you making?' she asked, slipping up onto a stool to watch as Rosa placed spoonfuls of mixture onto circles of pasta and then deftly folded and twisted them into little packets.

'Tortellini. Spinach and ricotta this time. Last time I made you chicken and mushroom, remember?'

'I remember! I loved it. You know, I never actually realised people made pasta from scratch.'

Rosa laughed. 'Most people don't bother.' She shrugged. 'Me, I love to cook and Dominic, he loves to eat. It works well. And now there is you to cook for too.'

'I'm putting on weight, you know. All this good food you're feeding me.'

The older woman nodded her approval. 'Then you are doing exactly what you're supposed to be doing.'

Angie watched her quick fingers flying for a while. 'I wish I could cook.'

Rosa's fingers stopped mid-parcel. 'Who says you can't cook?'

'I'm hopeless. Really. Never learnt and Shayne, my ex, he hated anything too fancy so there was no point.'

'I could teach you, if you like.'

'Really? You'd do that?'

'Of course! Come, you can start now. I'll show you what to do. Here, watch me…'

He heard the laughter long before he found the source. Good sense told him to turn away and head for his office or the workshop where he'd been spending plenty of evenings lately, but the sound defeated him. He hadn't heard laughter in this house for how long?

And he'd never heard her laugh.

What was so funny?

He found them in the kitchen, so absorbed in their task that they didn't notice him enter. They were concentrating now, Rosa showing Angelina something and Angelina, with flour on her hands, one of Rosa's pinnies tied around her and a pile of what looked like disasters alongside, was trying to copy her. A dollop of mixture, and then her fingers working furiously, her teeth biting her bottom lip in concentration. Until a triumphant, 'Ta da!' as she held the object aloft in her palm.

Across the room their eyes met, caught and froze and

Rosa stopped clapping and smiled. 'Dominic, you're home early for a change.'

'I have a late flight to Singapore. I came to pick up a few things.' He looked from one woman to the other.

'What are you doing?'

'Angelina's helping me make tortellini. Will you have time to eat before you go? I'll get some ready now if you like.'

He nodded his thanks to Rosa, took one final look at the thankfully mute woman standing by her side and made his exit, tugging on his tie as he went. He hadn't seen her since that night in his office. He'd kept his distance and she'd kept out of his way and it had proved this thing was possible. He'd known it would work out. In a house this size, there was no reason why they should bump into each other at all.

'Dominic?'

Then again…

He turned. She looked abashed. 'Sorry. Mr Pirelli.'

'Dominic is fine. It is my name.'

'Oh.' Her lips were pink, her cheeks were red, except for where she'd left a swipe of flour. He had to stop his hand from reaching out and wiping it off. 'Only if you're sure.'

'Of course I'm sure. As I will drop the Mrs Cameron and call you Angelina. I'm assuming Cameron is Shayne's name?'

She nodded, her teeth catching her bottom lip, some kind of paper dangling forgotten from her fingers.

'Then you don't need it. Angelina it is. And now I really must get moving, if that's all?'

'Mr Pirelli—Dominic. I wonder if you would do me a favour.'

He regarded her suspiciously, registering for the

first time that she wasn't wearing jeans; instead, had some kind of skirt on behind that apron. Nice ankles, he had time to register before he asked, 'What kind of favour?'

'I wondered if you could possibly be a referee for me.'

'What?'

'Only there's this job going at the local supermarket. I could use my old contacts, only it would look so much better coming from you.'

He turned away. 'No. No reference.'

She stopped him with a hand to his arm. 'Oh, but—'

He looked down at her pale fingers, wondered why something so cool-looking should feel so warm. 'Because you don't need a job. Don't I give you enough money?'

'It's not about the money.'

'Good. So we're agreed. You don't need a job.'

'No! It's about keeping busy. I'm bored, Dominic. There's nothing to do here but loll around by the pool and read books or magazines all day. I need something to do.'

He wasn't sure he was hearing her right. A woman was complaining about having nothing to do but lounge by the pool or go shopping? Carla had never complained about not having a job. Carla had never complained about not having anything to do. But he shoved thoughts of Carla away. At least he knew from what he'd seen and what Rosa had confirmed, she knew how to eat. 'You didn't sound bored when I walked in before.'

'Rosa took pity on me. She'll soon get sick of it. But if I had a job at the supermarket—'

'No.'

'It's only just around the corner—'

'Out of the question.'

'Just a few shifts a week—'

'Is there something wrong with your hearing? I said no!'

She stamped her foot. 'Then what am I supposed to do all day? What am I allowed to do by the lord and master of the house?'

He shrugged, half smiling to himself. Did she have any idea how cute she looked when she got angry and stamped her foot?

'Why not decorate the nursery, if you're so keen to keep busy?'

'The nursery?'

'I'll need somewhere for this baby when it's born.'

'But I don't… It's not… Dominic, it's not my place to organise your baby's nursery. It's not like it's my baby.'

He looked at her levelly, resenting the way she could so easily divorce herself from the child she carried as if it meant nothing to her. Wasn't she a woman? Surely she must have one maternal bone in her body? 'You wanted a job. I'm giving you one.'

Singapore was hot. Drenching. The negotiations over the sale of an office and shopping complex even more draining. But the buyers had wilted first, and he'd got his price and even an earlier flight home to Sydney. Now all he wanted was a shower and a cold beer and a chance to read the article he'd spied in a woman's magazine left on the seat next to him in the plane, not necessarily in that order.

He pulled the car up outside the garage. He'd put it away later on when he went down to the workshop after dinner. It relaxed him even when it frustrated him, and it frustrated him a lot. He still didn't know what he was doing, but he sensed he was getting better. Or maybe he just needed the escape.

A sound alerted him—a splash that hadn't come from the low swell on the rocks below. Someone was in the pool? Curious, he went to investigate, rounding the wall that screened off the pool area.

Someone *was* in the pool, submerged dolphin style halfway along the bottom. Angelina, he realised, with those long limbs, although it was hard to see anything more than two brief splashes of colour through the water. A few more underwater strokes and she neared the end, rising to the surface with a gasp. Not bad, he acknowledged. He knew what it took to get from one end of that pool to the other on one breath. Not bad at all.

And then she climbed out of the pool and his own breath was punched out of him. She was long and sleek and glowing wet, the bikini top struggling to cover her breasts, her upper arms slim rather than skinny now, even managing to look toned.

She'd put on weight, he realised approvingly. And as his gaze travelled down, he saw her belly, softly rounded, and felt a surge of masculine pride that was aeons old.

That was his child growing. His child swelling this woman's body and turning her lush like fruit ripening on a tree. As he watched, she turned her face up to the sun and squeezed the water from her hair, the action lifting her swelling breasts and emphasizing the long, fluid lines of her body.

God, but she looked sexy with his baby in her belly. And he was hit by a surge of lust so sudden and overwhelming that he had to force himself not to bridge the distance between them and snatch her up and bury himself in her long, sleek depths.

A moment later, appalled, he strode into the house. What the hell was wrong with him? How long had it been since he'd had sex? Clearly too long if he was starting to have fantasies about the likes of Mrs Cameron.

Rosa met him inside. 'Welcome home, Dominic. I trust everything went well. Is there anything you need?'

'A shower,' he said thickly, having no trouble working out the order he wanted things now, unable to meet Rosa's gaze in case the images he'd seen were still burned on his eyes for all to see. *A long cold shower.* 'That'll do for starters.'

CHAPTER EIGHT

HE WAS doing it all wrong. He was in his office, show-ered, with a cold beer in a frosted glass beside him, poring over the article.

He was only on page two of *Bonding with Your Unborn Baby*, but he didn't have to finish it to know he was doing it all wrong.

It was important, the experts advised, to start bonding with your child even before it was born. Women had an advantage over men, the article maintained, the bond developing naturally over the course of nine months of pregnancy. Women naturally connected with the baby sooner. Men had to make an effort.

He rubbed his jaw with one hand. He wasn't making an effort. He'd done everything he could in the last month to avoid contact with the woman who bore his child. Which might have been all right if Angelina was picking up the slack.

But she wasn't going to be around after the baby was born. She didn't even want a baby. She was the last person who was into forming bonds or making connec-tions. Hell, she was so not into this child that she hadn't even wanted to have anything to do with organising a nursery for it!

Which meant he had no choice. He was just going to

have to become more involved. It wasn't as if he couldn't survive the odd encounter with Angelina for his baby's sake. And he might as well start with organising the nursery.

'Do you have a list?' he asked as he steered the car onto the road.

'A long one. Not that you need everything now. Some things can wait.'

'Best to get it all now,' he said. 'Rosa will be too busy with the baby afterwards.'

'Rosa is going to be looking after the baby? Does Rosa know that?'

'It was her idea. Do you have a problem with that?'

She tried to suppress her objections. It wasn't her place to be concerned with how he intended to manage the care of a new baby with the hours he worked. But still… 'Rosa would do anything for you and you know it. But she already does so much. How's she supposed to manage the house and the cooking and a new baby?'

He glanced sideways at her. 'I thought you were happy to walk away. Why should you even care what happens after you're gone?'

'I don't care,' she huffed, tired of the direction the conversation was taking, blinking against the sun emerging from behind the dark cloud responsible for the last rain shower and now slanting through her window. 'You do what you like.' She tried to tell herself she didn't care. But he couldn't be serious, surely? There was no way he could expect Rosa to do all she did and lumber her with a new baby as well.

She tugged on her seat belt, releasing some of the tension so she could angle herself away from the sun, already intent on turning the damp road to steaming. She idly rubbed her belly with her free hand. She was more and more aware of her growing bump now and what it did and didn't like. Humidity it didn't.

She wasn't big by any means, but the changes in her body were a revelation. Every day she seemed to notice something new, a slight change in her shape or the fit of her clothes as her bump grew and her waist thickened.

'So who would have looked after this baby if it had been yours?'

She swung her head around. 'Me, of course.'

'But you never wanted a baby. That's what you told me.'

So what if she didn't? 'Is this actually relevant to anything?'

He shrugged, looked in his mirrors as the lane in front blocked up and smoothly changed gears and lanes in one fluid movement.

'Why did you marry him?'

'Did I miss a clause in that agreement I signed? The one that said you were entitled to know my deepest and darkest secrets, along with my most stupid mistakes.'

He flashed her a smile that made her bones turn to jelly and made her glad she was sitting down. He never smiled at her. He avoided her. And when he couldn't avoid her, he tolerated her. He didn't smile. 'Clause twenty-four, sub-clause C. You must have missed it.'

'Fine,' she said, still wilting under the combined effects of the sun and one devastating smile. 'In that case, it was my mother's fault.'

'You're blaming your mother for you marrying Shayne?'

'Yes. No. Well, sort of. We hadn't been going out long when we learned she was sick. He was good to me then—*good to us*—and my mother wanted to see me settled before she died. Wanted me to have the whole white wedding she'd never had. Shayne seemed keen.' She shrugged. 'It was the least I could do, under the circumstances.

'And it was okay. For a while.' She turned her head away. 'You know the rest.' She squeezed her eyes shut, expecting the pain and the prick of tears and wanting to hide her face before that happened, but surprisingly neither pain nor tears arrived. She exhaled a long, slow sigh of relief. Good. So maybe she was over feeling sorry for herself. Just as well, because by the lack of response, it looked like nobody else was interested. 'So that, in a nutshell, is the whole sad story. Are you asleep yet?'

'Not likely. Tell me, how did your mother die?'

She looked around, searching the high street shops lining the road, wanting a diversion if not an escape and wondering if it was fair to blame all her discomfort on the humidity. How far was this baby shop anyway? And why was he insisting she even do this? She didn't want to buy things for a baby she'd never know. She didn't want to lie in bed at night and imagine it lying in a tiny bassinet she'd chosen or wearing precious little outfits she'd selected.

Couldn't he see that? Couldn't he tell that she didn't want to know anything that would make it harder to forget this child?

And what was he even doing here? He'd shown no real interest in this baby, other than claiming ownership. He'd avoided her the last month and now he wanted to go nursery shopping? What was that about?

'Unless you don't want to tell me,' he prompted.

She put her head back against the headrest, closing her eyes. 'Breast cancer,' she said finally. 'By the time they found it...' She squeezed her lids tighter together, but this time there was no denying the pain or the tears that squeezed out, suddenly right back there, back at the restaurant and the celebration they'd all assumed it was.

'Mum treated us all for Christmas lunch, said she'd won some money on Lotto and wanted to splurge. She shouted us all—Shayne and me, his parents, even his sisters and their partners. I think she loved the idea of having a big family around her for once.' She paused. 'We'd never had a Christmas meal out before. It was such a treat to eat in a real restaurant. Everyone was wearing party hats and pulling Christmas crackers. It was the best Christmas we'd ever had.'

She dragged in air. She should have realised how tired her mother had looked, even as she'd so valiantly smiled and laughed and joined in. She should have noticed the shadows under her eyes and how little she had eaten herself while everyone around her was feasting. 'Mum made it a special Christmas for everyone. Until we got home and she confided to Shayne and me the truth. That she was dying. That she had only weeks to live and there was nothing anyone could do for her. The only thing she wanted more than anything was to know that her daughter would be taken care of.'

She took a deep breath, praying for strength to finish. Somehow she needed to finish, if only to explain how she could marry someone who could let her down so badly. 'We'd only been going out three months by then— when it came down to it we barely knew each other—but Shayne, to his damn credit and his eternal damnation, got down on his knee and proposed right then and there in front of her and what could I do? What could I say? I knew it was crazy and reckless but how could I say no to someone who wanted a dying woman's wish to come true? We were married a month later next to her hospital bed. Mum was my matron of honour.'

She dropped her head into her lap, one hand covering her mouth to cover the sobs she could no longer contain. 'We lost her the next day.'

Grief took her then. Grief for her loss. Grief for a well-intentioned but hasty and ill-conceived marriage. Grief for a lost mother and all those lost years. And then she felt his hand around hers, and this time it wasn't sparks she felt, but warmth and a jolt of connectivity as his fingers squeezed hers, his thumb stroking the back of her hand until the car jerked to a stop and he hauled her bodily against him. She tried to fight, she tried to push herself away, finally giving in when she knew she had no energy for the fight. No hope.

'She was the reason I was born at all!' She turned her head up to him through the curtain of her tears, uncaring of her swollen eyes and the mess she'd made of her face. 'My scumbag father wanted me aborted to avoid the responsibility of having a child. My grandparents wanted me aborted to avoid the shame of an illegitimate grandchild. My mother refused them all. She left everything and everyone she had once loved to protect me.'

Her sobs racked her slender body and he pulled her closer, surprised how easily, how comfortably, she fitted against him, how right it felt holding her.

She made another futile attempt to push away again but there was no way he was letting her go. 'I'm making you all wet,' she protested, and still he clung on.

How could he let her go? Because suddenly he understood. Suddenly it all made sense. He had never understood before why she had taken the stance she had, why she had refused her husband the solution the clinic had offered and that Shayne had demanded.

She herself had been given the opportunity to live.

So she would not take another's life.

And he didn't want to let her go.

He thought about the agreement, about the money he'd offered and the way she'd protested every step of the way and he finally realised why she would have done this for nothing. Finally he understood.

She deserved a thousand times more for doing what she was doing but she'd wanted nothing and he hadn't believed her.

Not completely. Not until now.

He held her while her sobs abated, while her breathing calmed. 'I'm so sorry,' she said. 'You didn't need to hear all that.'

'I think I did,' he told her, his lips brushing her hair, drinking in her scent. 'And now I understand. Now I know why you are such a special woman.'

She turned her face up to him and he saw the questions skate across the surface of her liquid eyes. Her face was flushed and tear-swept. There were mascara smudges at both eyes. He brushed a loose strand of hair from her face, stroked the pads of his fingers down her cheek and jaw, till they got to her chin and he could angle her face just the way he wanted. She looked so sad he wanted to kiss away her pain. Wanted to let her know he understood.

For a scant second he wondered at his actions. Once before he'd wanted to kiss her. He'd written off the impulse as an aberration. But it hadn't been an aberration, he now realised. It had been a necessity. An imperative.

One he wasn't about to let pass again. 'You are

special,' he told her, part because he suspected she needed to hear it, part because it was true and another part because he damned well wanted to. 'You are strong and beautiful and if I may say so, very, very alluring.'

Her gasp told him all he needed to know. She didn't believe it. Which meant that he would just have to convince her.

'Believe it,' he said, his lips coming closer, the first pass no more than a whisper of shared air and coiled expectation. Her lips followed his and he smiled. She wanted him. He wanted her to want him.

He knew this was right. Even here, sitting in a car in the midst of a nursery equipment warehouse car park in the middle of a busy day, he knew this was no aberration. This was right.

And this time his lips hesitated, hovered breathlessly above, until the need became urgent and the lure of her became too great. And then his lips met hers and he came undone.

His mouth meshed with hers, his fingers tangling in her hair and, like a man dying of thirst, he drank her in.

She was breathing hard when he broke off the kiss.

Breathing almost as hard as he was when he pulled away, his hands lining her jaw, his thumbs working the space between where her lips ended and her cheeks began. Her eyes were wide, brilliant blue and brimming with questions and wonder and fear. It was the fear that scared him the most, the fear that made him realise what he'd done.

'I'm sorry,' he said, letting her go. 'I shouldn't have done that.'

'It's okay,' she said, dabbing her eyes with a tissue,

still looking shell-shocked though he could see she was aiming for cool. 'I realise it didn't mean anything.'

He climbed from the car, rankled that she'd used the very words that would normally be uppermost in his mind. 'It meant something,' he said, pulling her door open a few moments later. 'It meant sorry for everything you've been through. It meant thank you for what you are doing. It meant thank you for telling me.'

'That's okay then,' she said, her composure returned though still wary enough to keep her distance as she climbed out. 'Maybe we should just forget it happened.' And she headed for the entrance.

Forget it happened? Forget the sweet taste of her mouth under his? Forget the way she felt so right in his arms?

How the hell was he supposed to do that?

The shop helped. Only it wasn't a shop, he decided, it was his worst nightmare. The place was acres across. How could anything as tiny as a baby warrant so much *stuff*?

'How do we do this quickly?' he asked.

She looked almost as overwhelmed. 'Maybe they have some kind of personal shopping consultant service.'

The notion appealed immensely. 'Let's find out,' he said, cutting a swathe through the crowds of couples inspecting prams and cots and baby gear to the service desk.

The woman was serving someone at the head of a line but still she looked up, as if some sixth sense had alerted her. Looked again when she saw what was approaching in his dark trousers and fitted cotton knit top.

Instantly her face lit up, and she shoved a bag in the direction of the customers she'd just put through the register so they could pack their purchases themselves.

He didn't need to jump the queue. 'Can I help you?' she asked, all bright-eyed and breathless in her eagerness to please.

'I need your help,' Dominic said in that ultra-deep voice, and the woman's eyes told them he could have whatever he wanted. 'You see, I'm having this baby and I don't have the first clue what I need. And all this...' he swept his arm in an arc around the showroom '...I have no time for this. Do you have some kind of consultancy service who can assist?'

Angie almost felt sorry for her. The woman was almost hyperventilating as he explained. He's not *that* special, she thought, and then she looked around at all the people in the store. There were a fair share of those who looked kind of normal, a few more who looked even better, and then, she had to concede, there was Dominic.

He was in a class of his own here. No wonder the woman was falling all over him.

'I can help,' she said, calling an assistant to take over her register. She stood to one side and smiled wanly at the next person waiting in line to check out their purchases, feeling guilty when she realised just how long the queue was.

Apparently they would all remain waiting until Dominic Pirelli's every need was satisfied. Strangely it was only the men who looked resentful. The women just looked hungry and, when they glanced her way, openly envious.

They'd look even more envious if they had any idea what they'd just been doing in the car. Angie trembled at the memories, remembering the way he had cradled her, comforting her, remembering how comfort had so quickly turned to something else. His lips had been surprisingly gentle, his taste had been addictive and there had been no way she'd been going to stop him.

What a fool. He'd kissed her because he felt sorry for her and she'd stupidly kissed him back as if he really meant it.

God, she was a fool!

She knew what he thought of her. She was the lowest of the low, from the back blocks of western Sydney, while he was a billionaire with a mansion on the sea. She'd seen his lip curl when they'd first met. She remembered the look on his face when he'd stepped inside her home, as if he was slumming it. She did not belong in his world and there was only one reason why she was here and it was not to be kissed by him or to kiss him, or to imagine this was some kind of fairy tale where they might all end up happily ever after.

Damn. She'd be every kind of fool if she thought that!

The consultant led the way, a clipboard on her arm with a list at least twice as long as Angie's. 'Your first baby?' she asked, and Angie had no doubt the woman didn't really care, she just wanted him to keep talking and enjoy the sensation of Dominic's deep voice rumbling through her bones again.

'It is,' was all he offered.

She sighed wistfully as she looked over her shoulder. 'I dare say it'll be a beautiful baby then, if it takes after you two.'

Dominic scowled and Angie squirmed. The woman was right, the baby would be beautiful, but it had nothing to do with her.

Thankfully, they arrived at the nursery decor section and the consultant got distracted. For the next hour they got lost in displays and colour schemes. Angie forced herself to think of it as a job, as Dominic had insisted it was. It had nothing to do with her. Not really. She was merely an onlooker here. She had to think of what this baby needed functionality wise—and not think of it as the baby growing inside her at all. The baby she wouldn't ever know...

She clamped down on the pointless pang of regret. She couldn't afford to think that way. She'd done the right thing, hadn't she? She'd reunited this child with its rightful father. She couldn't afford to have regrets.

Though it was getting harder and harder not to.

She looked around this massive baby warehouse, looked at all the people shopping for their child, for their baby. Envied them. For she'd never realised it would be this hard. She'd imagined handing the baby over would be easy. She'd never realised this stranger growing inside her would be so interesting or demand so much of her attention. She'd never realised it would make her feel as if it was truly part of her.

That it was hers...

Just for a moment she allowed herself to wonder what it would be like if things were different, if this baby were truly hers and she was shopping now with the most devastatingly handsome man in the store, if not in the whole of Sydney, for their child. How would that feel?

But no. She shook her head to clear the wayward thoughts away. There was no point going there. The reality was cold and hard and stared her in the face every time she remembered how he had treated her because of who she was and where she had come from. There was no place for fantasy here. She was merely a means to an end. An incubator for his baby. A temporary inconvenience.

'What do you think of this one?' Dominic interrupted

her thoughts with a picture of a brightly coloured themed room, filled with stuffed beanbags and a drum set and a red bed shaped like a Ferrari.

She blinked up at him. 'It's just a baby, Dominic. It might actually be a way off fast cars. And have you ever stopped to consider it might be a girl?'

He stared at her as if she were mad. 'Of course it's a boy.'

And he was so earnest she had to laugh. Finally, after poring over dozens of design books, they settled on a colour scheme. Walls of misty blue up to an animal frieze with the colour changing from blue to creamy clouds. White furniture, they decided, with accessories that would do for either boy or girl. After the baby arrived there would be plenty of time to add hints of colour.

Once the colour scheme was chosen, it was relatively easy. Furniture was selected to match the colour scheme and the existing decor of the house and meanwhile the list the consultant kept was getting longer and longer.

Dominic was having the time of his life. They'd covered bassinets and cots and bedding, made a brief foray into prams and strollers, and now they were looking at baths and changing tables. If this wasn't bonding with his baby, he didn't know what was. He lingered over a changing table that doubled as a baby bath and had drawers underneath for storage. The consultant assured him it was the epitome of efficiency. Efficiency he could relate to. He looked around to show Angelina but she was nowhere to be seen.

For a moment his gut clenched in fear. Where was she? How could he have lost her? And then he saw her in the clothing section a few metres away.

The tiny suit looked as if it had been made for a doll

rather than any baby she'd ever seen. Softer than velvet, the white fabric felt like a butterfly's kiss upon her skin. She smiled. The baby was bound to have its parents' colouring, bound to be born with a shock of dark hair and dark features.

Boy or girl, his baby would look gorgeous in white. *Not that she would ever know.*

The knowledge sliced through her like a knife and she hung the suit back on the rack. Now she was getting maudlin! It was pointless looking at clothes. Pointless thinking about how the baby might look. Pointless and painful. She swiped away a tear. She should never have come. She should never have let him make her. It was enough that she would be able to picture this baby's surroundings after it was born—its grand house, the seaside where it would grow up exploring the rocky shore. It was enough that she could already see Rosa feeding the toddler in a high chair in her massive kitchen. It was enough that she could see the baby being cradled against its father's chest…

'Did you find something?'

'No,' she said, sniffing back tears, moving away. 'Just looking.'

'Are you all right?' He looked at his watch. 'God, we've been here hours. You must be exhausted.'

The consultant watched on, concerned. 'I've got all your details. I can have this all delivered during the week if you like.'

It was exactly what he wanted to hear. 'Come back when you've had the baby,' the consultant called after he'd left his credit card details. 'We love seeing our happy families return.'

He was still scowling from that last comment when he opened her car door. 'What did you expect her to assume?' Angie said, relieved to be finished with the place, slipping her feet from her flats and pointing her toes. 'Of course they think we're a couple. Who else goes shopping in baby stores but pregnant women and their partners?'

Dominic said nothing. Just started the engine and turned on the air conditioning.

'Mind you, she was right about one thing.'

This time she got a bite. 'What do you mean?'

'This will be one beautiful baby. Carla was beautiful, Dominic. It's so unfair she didn't live to see her child.'

He didn't reply as he set the car in motion and she wished she'd said nothing too. He'd already be regretting that earlier kiss and now she'd gone and mentioned his wife. Not that he would need reminding of her. Did he feel he'd betrayed Carla, by kissing the woman carrying her child? Did he wish it was Carla sitting alongside him now? Did he wish it was Carla he'd been kissing?

Of course he would.

Instead he was stuck with her. But at least it was only for a few short months. And then he'd have Carla's baby and she would be free of pregnancy hormones and the crazy thoughts and fantasies they spawned that had no place in reality.

She could hardly wait.

He didn't go straight home as she'd expected. 'Where are we going?' she asked when she realised they were heading in the wrong direction.

'Do you have to rush back?' he asked enigmatically. 'I thought it might be nice to go for a drive now that the showers seem to have passed.'

She shrugged, surprised. There was nothing she had to get back for. But after that kiss she was sure he'd want to get her home and out of his hair as quickly as possible. Then again, he'd probably already forgotten about it. 'Sure.'

He pulled over and activated a switch that took the top down in a whirr of motor and click of machinery and soon the sports car was heading towards the city. Sydney almost sparkled in the sunlight as they crossed the Harbour Bridge, fresh from its earlier showers, a light on-shore breeze countering the humidity.

He seemed to know where he was going so she didn't bother him with questions. Just enjoyed the sensation of being in the passenger seat alongside him as they by-passed the city. She saw the looks of envy from the cars they passed, the men lusting after the car, the women lusting after Dominic.

He wasn't hers in any way, shape or form. A kiss did not bestow ownership by any means, especially one given in pity, and having his child in her belly did not make him hers, but she was the one sitting in this seat right now and she was going to enjoy it. She sat back and ate up the envy. Things would be different after the baby was born. Very different.

Already her former life seemed almost foreign. The little house she still didn't know if she would get to keep. The dusty streets and the baking heat. She would miss the clean smell of the ocean and the blazing sunrise as night turned to day.

But return she must. She'd signed an agreement to that effect, she'd sworn she'd leave as soon as the baby was born. It wasn't as if she had a choice.

And she didn't want to stay. Not really. Just like she'd never really wanted a baby...

The wind whipped over the windscreen, swirling over their heads, playing with the ends of her hair while reason tugged at the fraying ends of her mind. No, that wasn't quite right. She had wanted it—had thought that if she could give Shayne the baby he so desperately wanted that their marriage would finally become what her mother had wanted for her, what her mother had never had.

And for a moment, for just a few short weeks, she'd imagined her wishes had been answered and her hopes had been blessed. She hadn't known then that her marriage was already over.

And then they'd discovered the truth and relief had taken over. Massive relief. For it wasn't Shayne's baby she was carrying. It was Shayne's baby she didn't want.

But could she afford to want this one?

No. She'd never wanted this child. Never. And as long as she kept telling herself that, everything would be fine.

The car threaded its way through the inner suburbs, past the Sydney Cricket Ground and further on, past Randwick Racecourse. The car felt good in his hands and he felt good in it. It had been a while since he'd allowed himself the simple pleasure of taking one of his cars for a spin.

It had been a while since he'd wanted to show someone the simple delights of driving through the city streets with the top down.

He noticed the men he passed looking at them from their city-bound SUVs, enjoying their looks of envy when they saw the woman alongside him, the ends of her hair flicking in the breeze.

He couldn't blame them. She looked so different now from when he'd first met her. She'd gained weight in all the right places, her cheeks filled out now to balance that wide mouth and her long limbs toned from swimming and honey-gold from the sun. And he wondered how he could ever have taken her for anorexic.

He'd misjudged her in so many ways. She wasn't what he'd expected at all. She was—*more*.

At least she could be more. He remembered her reluctance to shop for the nursery. He remembered how upset she'd been in the store, as if it had all been such a chore and she couldn't wait to get away.

And none of it made sense because he also remembered how she'd felt in his arms, warm and yielding and womanly, her taste like a drug in his system...

He didn't like things not making sense. He didn't like it at all. Wondering what he was even doing here, he pulled the car into a just vacated space in the car park.

'This is it,' he announced, raising the top. 'Welcome to Coogee Beach.' Manicured lawns lined with Norfolk Island Pines on one side and the Pacific Ocean on the other spread out before them. 'Do you fancy a walk?'

She nodded, enjoying this rare chance for an outing despite the mess of conflicting thoughts in her head.

They wandered through the park, between the beach that was heaving with swimmers and the picnickers enjoying sizzling barbecues that sent delicious aromas into the air. They stopped for gelati before heading slowly up the path to the cliff walk. They paused at a lookout, gazing out at the surf and the ocean and the cruise ships and container vessels that ventured along the shipping lanes far out to sea.

'My mother used to bring me here,' he said, looking out towards the horizon, 'when I was just a child.' She looked up at him, at his tight expression, and she could see how much this cost him. 'My nonna and poppa—my grandparents—would come too. We would have picnics at the beach. Swim in the sea pools at first, and then in the surf when I was older. After a picnic we'd wander along the cliff walks and think how good it would be to live so close to the sea.'

And now he did. Their lives had been so different, she thought, gazing out over the magnificent stretch of coastline for the very first time. Cliffs and beach and tumbled rocks and salt-toughened bushes bursting with colour.

They gazed silently out to sea, watching the waves crash mightily on the rocks below, the white water spray going metres into the air, before the wave's energy dissipated, turning it to meek, foaming wash.

'When my grandparents died, it killed me,' he said, and she looked around to see his face so tight with pain it hurt her too. 'We didn't have much but we were a family. We had each other. Until a train collided with the bus they were in. They should have survived. I knew in my heart that my love for them should be enough to save them. If they'd been able to afford a car...'

She listened in silence, awed by the power and the pain of his words, fighting the urge to reach out and comfort him with his anguished face and his tightly bunched hands.

'For a while there was just my mother and me. We had each other. For a while—until once again I learned that love was nowhere near enough. That it was money you needed if you wanted things to happen. Money you needed in this world if you wanted to save and protect the ones you loved.' He turned to her then and it was all she could do not to reel away; his eyes were as black and bleak and empty of life as a bushfire-ravaged forest.

'Your mother died of cancer,' he said. 'Mine too. A brain tumour that sucked her of her life. And because we didn't have the money to pay for private treatment, we had to wait in line for months for her to have scans. Months to see a specialist. And by that time it was too late. There was nothing they could do. And I learned—by God I learned—that it is only money that can get you what you want, when you need it.'

His voice trailed off, carried away by the wind and the waves, and she thought he was spent until his voice came back, gravel-rich and thick with anguish as his gaze stayed firmly fixed on the shifting sea.

'Except I couldn't save Carla. All the money in the world, all the doctors and treatments and private hospitals and I couldn't save her. Nothing could save Carla.' He dragged in air. 'When you arrived, it was like the fates were laughing in my face, taunting me. And why if not to remind me how powerless I really was?

'I hated you then, hated what you represented, hated that you should turn up like you did and yet be claiming to carry my child.'

Waves crashed on the rocks below, seagulls wheeled in the sky and logic told her the world kept turning. But Angie could barely breathe for the tight bands wound around her heart and lungs.

'I was wrong, though. You're nothing like she was. I just thought you should know that. I was wrong and I'm sorry.'

He dropped his head onto his chest and dragged in a breath and finally turned his head towards her, his face devoid of expression. 'Let's go home.'

And he looked so defeated, so weary, that she didn't dare ask him the questions uppermost in her mind—questions about how Carla had died—couldn't put him through the agony of digging deeper into an obviously painful past. But as they made their way back to the car and through the streets of Sydney she absorbed what he had told her, not knowing why he had felt compelled today to tell her these things, but knowing that it helped her so much to make sense of the man—why he was driven the way he was. Why he needed so much to succeed in order to protect the ones he loved. What would that do to you, she wondered, if love had never worked in saving the people you loved, and then the money you'd thought would protect them hadn't either?

She shivered, the temperature turning noticeably cooler as clouds scudded over the sun. But even the cooler air wasn't enough to extinguish the tiny flickering flame his words had sparked inside her. He'd hated her once, as she'd known, but he didn't hate her now. And out of the firestorm of accusation and bitter emotion that had accompanied their first meeting had finally emerged a kernel of respect.

'You're nothing like she was.'

His words played over and over in her mind. If she didn't know how beautiful Carla had been, how perfect for Dominic she looked, she might almost have believed that was a good thing.

CHAPTER NINE

BONDING with the baby or bonding with Angelina? Dominic drove home not sure what had prompted his need to reveal so much about himself and his past, only that he knew to trust his gut sometimes, even when his head questioned his sanity. Besides, he owed her something for the assumptions he'd made when they'd met. She deserved at least some kind of explanation for that.

He came home from work the next day, a package under his arm. He found Angelina with Rosa in the kitchen, just as he'd suspected, a pile of sliced mushrooms on the bench between them with two big pots in readiness on the stove. It was a picture of domesticity he was still having trouble coming to terms with. The kitchen had been one of Carla's least favourite places.

'Good day?' he asked, helping himself to a slice of foccacia and dipping it into the dish of oil and balsamic vinegar alongside.

Angie looked up across the table and smiled. 'Rosa's teaching me how to make risotto. I think I'm beginning to get the hang of this cooking thing.'

'In fact, she's so good,' Rosa added, giving her

wooden spoon a flourish, 'I'm thinking of signing her up for the next round of *MasterChef.*'

'Hey,' Angelina protested, giving the older woman a playful smack on the arm with her own wooden spoon. 'That was supposed to be a secret!' Rosa laughed and dodged away.

He smiled, envying the easy camaraderie the two women had found in each other's company and the laughs that seemed to come so easily between them. The house felt a better place somehow, more alive since Angelina had arrived, especially lately. Definitely a stark contrast to the drama and tension-filled days that had been so much the hallmark of Carla's days here.

And Angelina herself had changed. Today she looked so happy, her eyes bright and bubbly, her colour high. She left her stool to check the pot on the stove and he realised she was wearing one of Rosa's pinnies again with just shorts and a strappy top underneath. He enjoyed the view from the back and that long stretch of legs, but then she turned and he could see nothing but white pinny and honey-gold limbs and he imagined it was how she would look if she was wearing nothing at all underneath.

Suddenly the pots weren't the only things simmering. He turned away, looking for something else to focus on, wondering what the hell was in the package under his arm until he remembered his plan. And in order to carry out that plan, the last thing he needed was to start imagining Angelina naked. Certainly not after that kiss and discovering how good she tasted.

It was the baby he was supposed to be bonding with, after all.

He grabbed a cold beer from the drinks fridge, willing its coolness south. 'I'll be down in the workshop if you need me. And Angelina?' She looked up, all blue-eyed innocence in a pinny he was having far less innocent thoughts about. 'I've got something to show you after dinner.'

He sat on the stool, his beer growing warm, Poppa's tools laid out on the bench before him. The wood was hard. The piece was challenging. But it was in there, he knew. And there was no way he wasn't going to find it.

'Mind if I join you?' She'd disappeared after dinner while he'd gone to check the markets, but Dominic found her in the ballroom of all places, with a chair pulled up close to a set of French windows and a pile of books stacked next to her, an open book on her lap. 'What are you doing? And why here?'

'I like it here,' she answered, sliding a bookmark between the pages and folding shut the book and inviting him to pull up a chair. 'I can see the sea but not burn to a crisp or get distracted by Sven the pool boy.'

He frowned. 'Since when did we have a pool boy called Sven?'

This time she did smile. 'That's my fantasy. You get your own.' He liked the smile. He liked that for once it was directed at him, even if she was laughing at him at the same time.

He glanced at the cover of the book she was reading, his eyes scanning the titles of the others in her pile. He felt himself frown. 'Those are all birthing books.'

'Go figure. I can't imagine why.' Her words were tart but there was another smile lurking there behind her own mock frown, he was convinced of it.

'Do you really need them, though?'

She blinked. 'I am having a baby, Dominic, in case you hadn't noticed.'

'Sure. But… Don't you… Surely… I mean, I didn't think you'd actually want to have it, if you know what I mean.'

She blinked again, shook her head. 'I don't think I'm following you. I just want to be prepared for what's going to happen.'

He finally pulled over a chair and sat down, putting down the package he'd brought with him while he ran the fingers of one hand through his hair. 'But why put yourself through the actual birth? Why go through all that pain and discomfort?'

'Because that's how women have babies?'

He shook his head; it made no sense to him. 'Wouldn't you rather have a Caesarean or something, though? So at least you can get organised?'

'You imagine Caesareans come without pain and discomfort?'

'But why do that to yourself?' God, Carla had been talking Caesarean from day one and that had been for her own child. A planned caesar, a personal trainer to get her back into shape, a plastic surgeon for the bits that refused to be trained. She'd had it all worked out. It wasn't as if he necessarily objected, but he just didn't understand. 'It's not like it's even your baby.'

She looked out to sea, at the rolling swell and the shifting diamonds sprinkled upon the surface of the water by the sun. No. It wasn't her baby. It had never been her baby.

But the more her body changed and the longer she harboured this other tiny life, the more she felt herself wishing that things could be different. 'I know,' she said on a sigh. 'Why don't we talk to the doctors about that?

I just don't want to take any unnecessary risks with this child, whoever it belongs to. Okay?'

He'd upset her, he could tell, but for the life of him, he couldn't work out why. He'd thought he was being considerate, thinking about her. He didn't expect her to go through hell to have his baby.

'Why did you come looking for me?'

'Oh.' He retrieved the parcel by his side, pulled out a stash of picture books. 'I went to a bookshop today. I wanted to get something I could read to the baby. To get it used to my voice before it's born. They say it can hear from a few months, maybe not quite yet, but given you are leaving, I should do something to bond with this child.'

God—she breathed in deep—did he have to remind her with every word, with every sentence? But he was right. 'That's a good idea. What did you get?'

He flicked through some of the titles. Most she recognised as classics. She stopped him when he got to *Possum Magic*. The Mem Fox book had been a favourite of hers when she was a child. She remembered her mother reading it to her at bed time. 'That one,' she said. 'Maybe you should start with that one.'

He looked a little uncertain, as if wondering if his idea was a mistake, so she just stared out of the windows so he wouldn't feel self-conscious and left it up to him.

'*Once upon a time*,' she heard, and already she was smiling. She knew the book practically by heart. She loved the story of Grandma Poss and Hush and the bush magic that made Hush invisible and the quest to make him visible again. She'd loved it when her mother had read it at bed time. And now, hearing the story come to life in Dominic's deep tones, she loved it even more.

This baby would so love bed times, she was sure. All too soon it was over. He finished the story, closed the book. 'Do you think it would be all right to do another one?'

She smiled and sat back in her chair and listened to him read *The Very Hungry Caterpillar* and *Time for Bed*, thinking she'd been so very wrong about Mr Dominic Pirelli and about how he cared about nothing except money, and how he might make an excellent father indeed.

And how this child might end up being so very, very lucky...

She felt the brush of something soft against her forehead. She felt the sway of movement. She stirred, wondering where she was, wondering why she felt so warm and safe when the ground was shifting below her.

And then she came to, to find herself in his arms. He smiled down at her. 'You fell asleep. Apparently, I tell a pretty effective bed time story.'

Half-asleep, she smiled back up at him, trying not to think too hard about how warm his body felt against her and how good it felt to be in his arms. 'You'll make one hell of a father.'

'You missed the last story,' he told her as he entered her suite.

'Which one was that?' She was sure she'd heard all of *Time for Bed*.

He laid her amongst the cloud-soft covers of her bed, kissed her softly on her brow. '*Tucking Mummy In*.'

They settled into somewhat of a routine after that. Dominic would leave early in the morning for the office. Angelina would walk along the cliff tops or swim in the pool and then she'd read or help Rosa during the day.

And after dinner Dominic would sit with Angelina and read to his baby. Sometimes picture books, sometimes longer chapter books, and she would sit and get lulled to sleep herself by the sound of his deep voice.

What she wouldn't give to be there to see this child listening to its father's voice, to see its tiny eyelids droop before it drifted into sleep.

But before she could get maudlin about what she would miss, the delivery van from the baby shop arrived, a truckload of purchases unloaded, including all the paint and paper she'd need to decorate the nursery.

And Angie put on overalls and headed for the nursery, amused by her own cunning. He wouldn't let her get a real job? Too bad. She'd make this one real in that case.

Rosa had arranged for the furniture to be removed from a small room nearest the master suite. The rest of it was up to Angie. It was the perfect room, with its own sitting room that would make a great play room, they'd all decided. Angie tried her hardest to stifle a concern that it was too far away from Rosa's room in case the baby cried, but Rosa calmly reminded her of the baby monitors they'd ordered and said it would all work out fine, so who was she to argue? Her job was to create the child a nursery.

Which was exactly what she was doing.

She spent the days cleaning the walls; she scrubbed the skirtings free of dust where they'd been hidden behind furniture. And then she prepped and painted.

The guaranteed toxic-free baby-safe paint went on like a dream. The colours were superb and with each layer she felt she was creating something special. This baby would have the best nursery ever.

By the time Dominic came home each night, she

would usually be found helping Rosa in the kitchen, baking bread or running fresh sheets of pasta through a machine to make fettucine.

'The decorators are taking a while,' he'd say, looking into pots and pinching an olive from the salad. And she'd murmur vaguely about paint colours with the wrong tint and conflicting jobs but they'd promised they'd be finished soon and Dominic would disappear a while before dinner down to the workshop.

'What does he do down there?' she asked Rosa one night when he'd once again taken himself off to the depths and she was busy pulling off basil leaves to dress the tomato and bocconcini salad. 'Tinker with those cars he keeps down there?'

The older woman shrugged and passed her the olive oil. 'Before you came he always used to disappear into his office. Now it's the garage.'

Before she came? A shiver went down her spine. 'Really? That's odd.'

Rosa nodded. 'And you know something else? Dominic never ventured into the kitchen before, except to say he was home.' She threw Angie a look that was loaded with meaning. 'He never dropped in to see what I was doing or to pick up a taste. Now what do you think is going on there?'

Angie didn't know. She didn't want to know. Didn't want to think too much about it.

But as she sprinkled oil over the top of the salad and ground on black pepper, she couldn't help but think about it.

Maybe whatever he was doing downstairs was giving his appetite an edge?

Maybe he was checking up on her, wanting to be sure

she was taking good care of his child? Now that one did make sense.

Or maybe…

Oh, no. She would not go anywhere near that *maybe*. To entertain that *maybe* was to invite despair and doom and utter humiliation on herself. There was no way he was attracted to her. No way he visited the kitchen for the pleasure of her company. The kiss had been a mistake. He'd said so. She'd agreed. It wouldn't happen again and it hadn't.

Not that knowing that hadn't stopped her dreaming of it every night.

She gasped when she felt it, so deep in thought that the tiny flutter caught her unawares.

'What is it?' said Rosa. 'Are you all right?'

And a smile found its way to her lips, a sense of wonderment overwhelming her as her palm cupped her bump. 'I felt it, Rosa. I felt it moving. It must still just be tiny but I felt it move.'

Rosa squeezed her shoulders in a hug. 'It is a feeling like no other. Your baby is playing. And just wait until he starts with the football. Then you will know you are alive.'

'I never realised…' she whispered, still awed by the concept of this tiny baby active inside her. Never realised the magnitude of the emotions she would feel, never realised the sheer wonder at the miracle that was taking place inside her, part of her but not belonging.

Never realised that she would feel this bond with a child that wasn't hers.

And it terrified her.

'I'm flying to Auckland tomorrow,' he revealed a couple of nights later as Rosa served dinner. The instructions were ostensibly meant for Rosa's planning purposes but Angie hung on to every word. 'I'll be there a week.'

So long...

Then again, an entire week? She could put in longer days and have the nursery finished by then. The furniture could be in place. She could show him what she'd done.

She couldn't wait to show him what she'd done.

'Simone's coming with me this time—a couple of functions I have to attend. All good PR. But she won't be around if you need to contact me urgently so best to call me direct.'

Rosa flashed a glance in Angie's direction but Angie just smiled, doing her level best to look unconcerned, wondering where this sudden coiling thread of jealousy had come from. And why should she feel jealous?

Simone was his beautiful, elegant PA while Angie was doing nothing more than carrying his child. She was an incubator. She had no claims on Dominic. It wasn't as if she had any right to feel jealous of the woman spending days and nights away with the father of her child. Not when she was his PA, for heaven's sake!

She would miss him because of the effort he was making with his baby. She would miss him because his baby would no doubt miss him.

It was hardly as if she were in love with him.

Liar, a small voice sounded.

She couldn't be in love with him.

Get used to it, she heard the voice say. *Why else are you so jealous?*

She hated that voice. Hated what it was telling her. *Hated more than anything that she suspected it was right.*

She sniffed. He was taking Simone away with him. Why shouldn't she be jealous?

The woman was beautiful. Sleek, dark-haired and gorgeous, just like his first wife. How could he not be attracted to her? How could he not choose her to be his life partner?

And now they had a week away together. Damn it all, she didn't want Dominic to marry someone like Simone. He had a baby to think about—a tiny baby who would need a mother. *This baby*. And Simone had struck her as someone as maternal as a viper. Surely he could find someone altogether more…*nurturing*?

She heard her name. Looked around to see piercing dark eyes following her fork, which was tracking idly around the edge of her spaghetti. 'You're not eating.' He was watching her carefully. Closely.

She pushed the bowl away. 'I'm not very hungry.'

His frown deepened. 'You're not sick?'

Heart-sick. Devastated. Green with jealousy. And shell-shocked beyond belief. 'I'm fine.'

If he believed her it didn't show. 'So your scan. I won't miss it?'

She searched through her shattered thoughts for his meaning, remembering the appointment for her twenty-week scan. Twenty weeks already. Which meant twenty weeks until the birth. Twenty weeks until it was time for her to leave. *So soon.* She shook her head. 'It's not till the twenty-first. But I wasn't expecting you to come with me.'

The look he sent her was one hundred per cent owner-ship, one hundred per cent proprietorial, and all clad in black-as-night eyes that she would miss more than she wanted to admit when she was gone. 'I'll be there.'

* * *

Auckland was a grind. Normally he thrived on the cut and thrust of doing business face to face. Normally he relished the challenge of negotiating and securing a deal. But here he'd endured meetings that had gone around and around in circles; he'd spent hours locked away in offices in negotiations and he'd suffered long lunches and long dinners, where Simone had been the only person who understood. Stoic Simone who had stayed by his side and said all the right things and smiled to all the right people and laughed at all the lame jokes.

Thankfully, it was the last night. One formal reception and he could escape. He studded cufflinks through shirt cuffs, wondering if he really needed to be here, wondering how things were at home.

Wondering if he'd notice any changes in Angelina's shape when he got back.

Angelina.

The name suited her so well. It hadn't at first, when she'd been merely Angie. The name had seemed wrong to him then. But Angelina. That was her. Long limbed and lithe, her sun-kissed hair layered around her face, her lips wide and lush, her eyes so blue he was tempted to dive right into their depths.

A picture flashed into his mind. Angelina standing by the pool, her hands in her hair, her skin honey-gold from the sun and her breasts like an invitation. And lust speared into him again, just as it had that day, hot and hard.

Damn. He grabbed his jacket and frowned, wondering just when it was that he'd stopped thinking of her merely as an incubator and more as a woman? And why now, when he had an evening of dreariness right here to look forward to?

Maybe because you've never had any reason to look

forward to going home before, said a small voice in his head. *Because when Carla was there…*

He shrugged the jacket on and just as easily shrugged those thoughts away. Carla was gone. Never again would he make that mistake. Never again would he fall for a woman who was so shallow.

Angelina wasn't shallow. Angelina was there now. *Angelina and his child.*

And deciding he wasn't really needed here wasn't such a difficult decision to make at all.

The room was perfect. Almost perfect, Angie realised, as she noticed the row of teddy bears lining the floor instead of sitting atop the shelf that had been purpose-built for them. Darn, how had she missed them?

She snagged a bunch of teddies under one arm and dragged a nearby chair. The bears were an easy fix although the chair could do with being a few inches higher. She was up there on the chair, stretching high to place them. She loved the bears. She loved their faces, some hand-stitched, some machined, but all of them with some kind of expression. She loved them all.

'What the hell do you think you're doing?'

She turned too fast at the booming voice—he wasn't supposed to be home yet—lost her balance and she and the remaining teddies went spinning into space.

He caught her, although crashing into someone as hard as Dominic, she figured, as the air was knocked from her lungs, was surely every bit as hard as crashing to the ground. 'What kind of stupid idea was that?'

'I'll say.' She found her feet, willing her breathing and her pulse back to normal. Not that that was likely given he still held her in his arms. 'What on earth made you yell like that?'

'You were up on the chair!'

'I know. And I was perfectly fine until you barged in huffing more steam than a locomotive.'

'But you were up on the chair!'

'I was there, remember, safe as houses until you exploded onto the scene.'

'Are you all right?' He held her shoulders and looked her over. 'Is the baby all right?'

'The baby's fine.' It was her who was finding it difficult to breathe. His big hands were warm on her shoulders and did he realise his thumbs were stroking her skin and doing all sorts of weird things to her breathing, not to mention her nipples?

But it was good to see him. She drank him in. The dark, tousled hair, black-as-night eyes and chiselled jaw. And then he finished his inspection and looked into her eyes and she nearly melted. And it was all she could do to get out the words.

'Welcome home.'

Her simple welcome was a balm to the soul. His hands shifted. Slowly, subtly as he looked at her, but inexorably towards the column of her throat. He sensed her breath hitch, he saw the fluttering heartbeat at her neck, watched her pupils dilate.

His fingers splayed in her hair as he drew her closer, steered her lips against his own and drank in her sweet essence as he kissed her long and deep. *Welcome home.* Oh, yeah. *This* was a welcome home.

Her taste was addictive. Irresistible. It wasn't enough. He wanted all of her.

His hands brought her closer until her breasts met his chest and her bump met his aching hardness and he could find a way to say what he needed to say.

'I want you,' he told her. 'I don't know why. I know

it's probably wrong or immoral or unethical or all of the above, but I want you and I know that if I kiss you again there is no way I'm going to be able to stop without making love to every single part of you. And even if I don't kiss you, it's what I want.'

She made a small sound—a whimper—and he was afraid that she was halfway to raising an objection, telling him he was crazy and about to go running and screaming for the hills. But she didn't pull away, made no attempt to go running screaming for the hills, her blue eyes looking up at him with what looked like wonder.

'You're beautiful,' he whispered as he brought her forehead to his lips for a kiss. 'Let me make love to you.'

She paused—a moment in time, she knew, had never felt so rich and agonizingly beautiful.

'I'm afraid,' she whispered, trembling into his arms.

He kissed her cheeks. Her eyes. Her nose.

So am I, he heard, the words coming from the cracks in the stone that was his heart. *So am I.*

But he said nothing. He just kissed her and swung her into his arms. Lust, he told himself, trying to reassure himself, plastering over the cracks while he carried her to his room next door. Pure animal lust.

Absolutely nothing to be afraid of.

He placed her reverentially on the bed. Along with Rosa's cooking, his big bed was one of his favourite things when he came home from business trips. Now, with Angelina lying on the covers, her chest rapidly rising and falling, her cheeks pink, her hair like a golden halo against his dark cotton, the bed shot straight to the top of the list.

Oh, God.

He wanted to be able to go slow except he didn't know if he could. He knelt down next to her and dipped his head, unable to resist the lure of that wide mouth and those parted lips, unable to stop himself from exploring her with one hand. The dip of her waist, the flare of her hip, the curving tightness of her belly. Everywhere his hands found magic, every part of her a joy, and when he cupped one breast, brushed one peaked nipple with his thumb and felt her mewl of pleasure in his mouth, he felt a primal surge of pride.

He loved the sundress she was wearing, loved that he could slide the fabric up her long, smooth legs, loved that he could take his hand all the way to the sweet curve of her behind with nothing to stop him on the long slide north to paradise. She shuddered into his mouth, trembled with want under his hands and arched into his touch.

Take it slow? She was killing him. His blood thundered in his veins as he found a zip, slid it down, manoeuvred her out of the dress and damn near came when he gazed down at her.

She was beautiful. Long limbs. Glorious breasts he would delight in liberating from a plain white bra, her breasts somehow turned into wicked temptation. And his baby stretching her belly.

He shrugged off his shirt and she shuddered as she watched hungrily and he knew she was on as tight a knife-edge as he was. And then he undid his trousers and he saw her eyes follow his hands and widen in an age-old feminine sign of approval as he kicked them away.

'Dominic,' she uttered breathlessly as his underwear joined them and he joined her back on the bed with a kiss that blew his mind. Skin against skin. Was there any better sensation in the world?

No, he decided, as he peeled her straps down her arms with his teeth and released her breasts to his gaze, his hands, his hot mouth. She cried out when he took their pebbled peaks between his lips; her hands clawed at him, clung to him, her need rivalling his own.

No, he decided, as his tongue trailed lower, to the swell of her belly. He put his lips to her bump, a kiss for the baby that grew beneath, a kiss for the woman who would give him this child.

No, he decided as he moved down the majesty of her ripening body, gently lowering her underwear from her hips, revealing her most secret place to his gaze, his hands at her thighs, stroking, relishing. No better feeling.

She moaned, a low soft moan that called to his inner beast and he dropped his head, parted her gently and supped on her. Her hands tangled in his hair, her body bucking, her gasps coming quick and fast as his tongue destroyed what defences she had left and laid waste to her.

And then she tensed under him, tensed for that sweet second, poised on the brink of the point of no return, before a flick of his tongue catapulted her over and she came apart in his mouth. And he somehow managed to smile under the weight of his own need for release. Somehow watching her come had been more satisfying than he'd imagined. He could wait.

She couldn't breathe. Couldn't think. But oh, how she could feel! Every part of her was alight, every part of her sang with pleasure and then he joined her, his kiss deep and drugging, a kiss that tasted of him and tasted of her and the thought of that was enough to ignite her senses all over again.

'I have to have you.' The words sounded as if they'd been ground through his teeth. He splayed a hand over her belly. 'I will try to be gentle.'

'The baby is fine,' she whispered. *It is me who will get hurt.* And the hurt would come, she knew. The hurt and the regret and the sorrow. But there was time for that later. A lifetime for sorrow. And right now there was no room for hurt. There was only time to feel.

'You are so unbelievably sexy,' he whispered, his lips against her breast, his tongue flicking at a nipple. His words stirred her, his voice husky and rich, brushing over her skin and senses like a velvet rasp. He was the magnificent one, broad-chested, lean and powerful, all muscle and corded strength, and he was calling her sexy?

And then she felt him. *There.*

He was so big. A momentary fear gripped her and held on tight. It had been a while. Months. And even then...

But then he pulled her into another of those kisses with that tongue that seemed to reach right in and rip her very soul from her body and she forgot everything except how to feel.

And how he made her feel.

He entered her in a thrust that made her gasp and sent her head driving back into the pillows, her back arching as her body stretched to accommodate him.

Time stood still while they lay joined. Fused.

And then he moaned above her, a low moan that sounded as if it had been ground through his teeth and spoke restraint that was being sorely tested, and slowly withdrew. She clung to him, desperate to keep him there, using all her muscles to contain him, the slide of his skin against hers a delicious friction, the feel of him poised once again at her entrance an exquisite torture.

She tilted her hips and he groaned again, this cry more desperate, his need matching her own, before he lunged into her, deeper this time, impossibly better.

She was gasping now, wild with need as he moved inside her, building the rhythm, his kisses pulling her deeper, his mouth hot and hungry, his big hands on her breasts, at her hips, setting her skin alight wherever he made contact.

Slick and hard, he filled her. Stretched her. *Completed her.*

Colours were her new friends. Colours that sparked behind her eyelids, colours that shot fireworks searing through her senses.

She could not come again. Somewhere in the vague recesses of her mind she knew that. Not twice in one night. It had never happened before. It couldn't happen now. But still the colours flashed, the sensations mounted and denial slowly turned into a smouldering sense of wonderment, a rising tide of tension, a need that went beyond mere completion. A need that demanded his completion too.

He drove into her, his sculpted back slick beneath her hands, every muscle tight and taut with that skin straining, every last part of him focused and true, until the smoulder became a curling ripple of smoke that became a raging fire that sent clouds to obliterate the sun.

With one final thrust he set her alight, her senses exploding, shorting, fusing as she came. She burned up in the inferno he'd triggered inside her. She lost herself in the flames. And she wondered, vaguely, from a very,

very long way away, if she would ever really find herself again.

Later, much later, she left him while he slept, lifted his arm from her body and eased herself away. It was late in the afternoon. Rosa would wonder why she wasn't in the kitchen—if she came to the nursery looking and found her like this, Angie would never live it down. Worse, she couldn't bear it if Dominic woke and she saw the resentment return to those dark eyes. She couldn't bear to be there when he realised what a mistake he'd made.

For it was a mistake, she should know. From the moment of her conception her entire life had been based on mistakes.

An unplanned pregnancy, an ill-conceived wedding, a wrong embryo. A mistake had brought her to Dominic's home and now another mistake had seen her fall into his bed.

When would she ever learn?

She located her clothes, slipped on her crumpled dress, smoothing it down her legs. She spared him one last lingering glance, admiring the sheer unadulterated magnificence of the man—this was one mistake that would haunt her for the rest of her life.

And fled.

She was gone, his bed empty when he woke and reached for her, hungry for her again. Her scent lingered on the pillow, fresh and feminine, taunting him in her absence as the soft light of dusk filtered through the curtains.

Just lust, he told himself, sinking back into the pillows. It was probably for the best that she had gone. It had probably saved them both some awkward moments.

Just sex.

He growled and pushed himself from the bed, striding to the bathroom.

Just sex? Was that how she saw it? She'd been molten in his hands. He'd taken her apart and put her together and taken her apart again. She hadn't been faking it. He was too good at what he did not to recognise that.

And she'd just walked away.

Maybe it was better. Maybe she was right.

She was going to leave anyway.

Maybe it would make things less complicated.

He snapped on the shower, stepped in while the water was still cold and growled again as he put his face up into the spray.

But there were weeks to go before she left, he told himself, and he wasn't done with lust just yet.

CHAPTER TEN

THE clinic was cool and welcoming as they entered, as only health practices could be. But it never ceased to amaze her that for a place promoting fertility, it managed to maintain such a sterile atmosphere.

Dominic walked stiffly by her side, his eyes still hidden under sunglasses, and Angie imagined his eyes beneath, unblinking and unforgiving.

But she could understand why his mood would suddenly darken, for this was the very same place that had offered her the option of getting rid of his child.

Maybe that was why he was here like a dark cloud to accompany her. Because he didn't trust them. *Welcome to the club*, she thought, groaning a little, her bladder full to bursting point. If the clinic was running late, she might just explode right there in the waiting room.

But there was no waiting. Within ten minutes she was gowned up and lying on the examination table with towels strategically placed. Then her gown was pulled up and her belly exposed and gelled. The probe pressed into her swollen tummy, pressure she didn't need, but she was distracted by Dominic by her side, the dark cloud vanquished, now looking agonisingly anxious as he was asked to be patient for a few minutes before the monitor could be turned.

Dominic patient? She smiled at the contradiction in terms, smiled at his furrowed brow and dark, worried eyes.

He really cares, she thought, as the man she'd thought a mountain looked achingly vulnerable and for a moment, just a moment, she wished he cared that way for her, not merely for the unborn child inside her.

And jealousy snaked its twisted way through her heart. For this was Carla's baby he was concerned for. This was Carla's baby he wanted—the baby she'd never been able to have. Carla—the woman he had loved and lost.

And so help her, but she was jealous of her. Jealous of a dead woman. What kind of woman was she?

Tears pricked at her eyes as she uttered a silent apology to the innocent child lying inside her. Whatever else happened, at least she had been able to do this for him. For them both. At least she had been able to give him Carla's child.

'Is everything all right?' he asked, his patience wearing thin.

The radiographer smiled. 'Everything looks perfect. Your baby is doing everything right. I'll show you in a moment. Do you want to find out what sex it is?'

The question hung in the air, and beside her Dominic asked, 'What do you think?'

The question was so unexpected, it winded her. He was asking her? She didn't care, did she? She wasn't supposed to care or have an opinion. It was a baby. That was all she needed or wanted to know. Besides, did it matter? Surely any child of Dominic's would be a gift, boy or girl…

'It's your baby, Dominic. It's your choice.'

And he looked down at her, his eyes studying her face, questioning. 'No,' he decided. 'Don't tell us.'

The doctor nodded and the radiographer swivelled the screen so they could see. Angie studied her feet. She'd found the six-week scan amazing. There was her baby, she'd thought, a tiny jelly bean with a heartbeat. She'd been fascinated by the tiny life, simultaneously racked with guilt that she had never really wanted a child, terrified at the thought she wouldn't love it enough.

But the baby had never been hers and it had been a strange, sweet relief she'd felt to discover that. Escape.

The men's voices washed over her while she lay there, terrified all over again. The fascination was there—it was impossible to deny that part of her that wondered what this creature looked like, this thing growing inside her that treated her more and more to night time jabs and swishing tumbles that caught her unawares and took her breath away.

But the fear was back, bigger than ever. This time not that she would not love this child.

But that she would.

Her nerve-endings tingled with fear. She could not afford to love this child. She'd only managed to decorate the nursery out of sheer bloody-mindedness at Dominic not letting her get a job. She'd only managed by thinking of the baby as an abstract, not connecting it with this child contained within.

She could not afford to see it.

She could not afford to want it.

As far as she was concerned, this was merely a package she was delivering. A gift, if it came to that. It was never hers to keep.

'Look, Angelina, can you see from there?' The sheer

joy in Dominic's voice broke through her thoughts. 'The baby's sucking its thumb!'

And in spite of herself, in spite of the fear, Angie looked then, wanting to be part of his discovery, envying his joy. The picture was indistinct, shades of grey fading in and out, but she found sense in the shadows, and shape and even definition. And she found something else too as she gazed at the unborn child, something she'd been terrified of.

A yearning for that which could not be hers. She suddenly wanted the months to fly by so she could cradle the tiny infant in her arms, to kiss its soft downy cheek and hold it to her breast.

To be its mother.

'Beautiful,' he said, his rich voice gravelly thick and filled with awe and wonder and she looked at him, his gaze intent on the screen, his dark eyes filled with emotion as he drank in the features of his unborn child, and she knew she was dreaming.

For she was nothing to him but a means to an end.

The baby was the thing he wanted, the thing he craved.

She was disposable.

And she had no right to yearn.

With a sigh she realised it was good she'd left his bed when she had, while she'd still been capable of it. Good she'd pulled back and created some distance between them. Good that she'd let him go before he'd done the same to her.

And he would have let her go, nothing surer. Men like him didn't fall for women like her. They fell for sleek high-gloss sirens who could further their career, not charity cases from the back blocks. Besides, he'd made no attempt since that night to come to her. Wasn't that proof he was regretting that night as much as her? No, it was clear she'd done the right thing.

And if she managed to keep her distance, she might even just survive this with her pride, if not her heart, intact.

She was quiet on the way home, barely saying a word in response to his attempts at conversation. He'd expected her to be a little shy given the last time they'd tangled words they'd ended up tangled together in the sheets, something he was having trouble getting out of his head, but it was more than that.

She was cool, distant, and so he hadn't bothered making too many attempts at conversation. For it had soon become clear she didn't share his excitement over what they had witnessed on the scan.

He was disappointed. He'd thought she'd at least express some interest in the child she was carrying. He'd thought he'd seen some flicker of maternal instinct in her expression in the way she'd curve her hand under her bump, rubbing it gently, whispering soft words when she thought he wasn't looking. And what about what she'd done in preparing the nursery! It had been Rosa who had disclosed that Angelina had done it all herself—all of it. How could a woman prepare rooms for an infant like that and not be interested in seeing that infant's face on a screen?

Was she really so opposed to the idea of having a child?

Perhaps she was.

But perhaps that was what it took to be able to walk away. Right from the start she'd insisted she wanted no part in it, that she would walk away and never have anything to do with the child again. Right from the start she'd told him she wouldn't change her mind.

It appeared that she wouldn't.

Which was a shame, really.

He'd been thinking lately about what she'd said about Rosa managing an infant along with the house. Rosa would be happy to do it, he knew, but it was unfair to expect her to. He hadn't given it enough thought. And down there in the garage last night, sculpting the piece he was working on, thinking about this woman splayed across his big bed, a look of utter abandonment on her face when he'd sent her plunging over the abyss for a second time and how much he burned to send her to oblivion again, the kernel of an idea had come to him. A good idea, he'd thought. A sensible solution.

Though clearly it would never work. Not once she found out what he had managed to secure for her.

Shame.

Dinner would have been completely silent if not for the occasional unintended clatter and scrape of cutlery against crockery, and even that rare occurrence intruded into the otherwise quiet. Rosa gathered the unfinished plates, saying nothing yet saying volumes in her eyes. Across the table Dominic sat like a volcano, brooding and about to erupt.

Angelina didn't dare look at his eyes. She said no to dessert, despite the fact she'd barely touched her dinner, and when Dominic called her back, halfway to leaving, she expected he was going to admonish her for not eating all her meal.

'I have something for you,' he said instead. 'Meet me in my office in ten minutes.'

She almost breathed a sigh of relief. The old Dominic was back. The old Dominic she could deal with.

Duly she arrived at his office at the appointed time, expecting the worst. He was waiting for her, standing stiff and tall and mountainous behind his desk. 'What did you want to see me about?' Try as she might, it was impossible to keep the slight tremor from her voice.

His face looked like thunder, his stance so tightly drawn she wondered if he might snap if he so much as moved. But he did move, picking up some documents on his desk, handing them to her. 'These belong to you, I believe.'

Confused, she took them and tried to make sense of what she was holding. She blinked, not entirely recognising the property reference, still unsure what it all meant when she saw the mortgage discharged stamp on the second page. A sizzling snake wound its way up her spine. She looked up at him. 'Is this what I think it is?' He was waiting. She imagined he wasn't used to people not understanding forms and papers and legal things, but she'd never seen a title deed before, if this was what it was.

'It's the title deed to your house on Spinifex Avenue. It's yours now, lock stock and barrel.'

His words confirmed her wildest imaginings. 'It's mine! But what about Shayne? What happened? I thought he wanted his so-called share.'

He snorted with contempt. 'The lawyers sorted that. In the end, as we suspected, he was happy to settle.'

'But who paid him? Who paid the mortgage out?'

He brushed her questions aside. 'Forget it—he came cheap. The mortgage even cheaper. I figured it was the least I could do.'

The least he could do when he'd already done so

much? She looked down at the deeds, unable to believe what she was seeing. The house was hers. All hers. It was a dream come true.

Except...

Wanting the house belonged to a different dream. A dream that belonged to a different time, when she'd willingly go home after the birth. Willingly go home, alone.

A wave of logic swept her objections away. Because it didn't matter what she thought or what she wanted or whether she was having second thoughts.

Dominic was only doing this because Dominic wanted her gone and she'd agreed that was what she would do. Was that so surprising? He'd always wanted her gone. He'd always expected her to leave. That was their arrangement, after all. Now he was doing everything possible to make it happen. And she would need somewhere to live.

Could she blame him for inadvertently making her life more difficult when he'd only just given her what she'd claimed she'd wanted all along?

Or should she thank him and not reveal how much his kind gesture was costing her when her mother's house was the only lifeline she could trust?

'Thank you,' she said at last, hugging the title deeds to her chest.

The night was hot, the sheets were tangled and the baby had put on soccer boots. Angie decided to give up on trying to sleep for a while. Besides, did she really want to sleep when all she dreamed about lately was Dominic? He'd been so good to her. Too good, really. He'd spoiled her for anyone else, that was for sure. And now tonight, giving her the deeds for her house... How did you thank someone for doing that, for being so thoughtful, even when you longed for another outcome?

She stood by the windows looking out to sea, trying to catch a breeze, but the night was strangely silent, the sea calm and quiet, with nothing to stir even a ripple through the foliage.

Below her window the moon reflected off the surface of the pool. A swim would cool her heated body. A swim might even cool her heated desires, and that would be welcome, for she'd found it impossible to live in the same house as this man and not have heated desires. She glanced at the time. Insanely late. Nobody would be awake now. Nobody would see her. And a soak would relax her, she knew.

She put on the bikini she'd bought with Antonia, noticing how much more of her bump escaped between top and bottom now, and how little of her breasts the top covered, and dragged out one of her old singlet tops and put that over the top. There. Almost decent.

And then she grabbed a towel and padded through the sleeping house, heading for the pool.

The water was cool without being cold and Angie sighed as she slipped into its welcoming depths. It was bliss against her heated flesh.

She breast-stroked quietly across the pool, relishing the support it lent and the cool slip of water against her skin. She tingled with pleasure, reminding her of another sensual night, another's sensual touch. Tremors bloomed inside her at the memories, just thinking about his big hands and how they'd felt on her body. Possessive. Deliberate.

She missed them.

Halfway back, her singlet bothered her, tight and heavy and dragging with the weight of the water she wanted against her breasts, and out here, alone, she decided she didn't need it. She tugged it off, tossing it the side, where it landed with a slap on the stone surrounds, and resumed her slow, gentle strokes. The water whispered past her breasts, sensual currents making her nipples peak and turning alight skin already sensitised by memories that could not be erased.

She reached the deep end and stopped, resting her arms on the edge, dangling her legs through the water, feeling suddenly frustrated. So much for a cooling dip. This wasn't working at all.

Dominic was still in the garage, wondering why he felt the need to continue with the piece at all. It was torture now, working the piece, shaping it, recreating from memory the scale and the curves. And every time he touched it, every time he turned it in his hands, it made him think of her.

He had to finish it, if for no other reason than to stop thinking of her. Besides, he had a bin full of abandoned projects. This one, he knew, he had no choice but to persist with until the bitter end. He glanced at the watch he'd set close to his forgotten and now cold cup of coffee and winced, knowing he had to be up in a few short hours and remembering he'd wanted to do some work on the overseas markets before he went to bed.

Which pretty much meant now if it was going to happen at all. He took one last look at the sculpture, committing it to memory so his subconscious could work on what he needed to do tomorrow, and snapped off the lamp.

The night was quiet and heavy with it, a change expected tomorrow that would liven things up weather-wise. But, for now, the warm night air was eerily silent as he stretched his legs outside under the moon before heading upstairs. He heard it then, no more than a burble, a swish of water and the hint of a sigh that had him turning rock-hard even before he turned towards the pool.

Surely not?

Night time fantasies were just that, weren't they?

And then he heard a wet slap and saw her in the pool, her bare arms pearlescent under the light of the moon, and fantasy collided with reality.

And he didn't care that he'd decided it would be better to stay away. He didn't care if he knew she didn't want his child, because there was no way he could turn away. Because, he thought, as the top button came undone, and the next followed, this wasn't about any child, or about what he knew was good for him.

This was about wanting her.

Pure unadulterated need.

And it was killing him.

She heard his footsteps before the husky, deep, 'Hot night, mind if I join you?'

She swallowed. His shirt was already undone, a column of superb masculine flesh exposed to her gaze from his neck to his waist. Skin her fingers ached to touch. 'It's your pool,' she managed. 'Although you're not exactly dressed for it.'

'Easy fix,' he said, his hands at his belt as he kicked off his shoes.

She turned her head away, wanting to look but afraid to, wondering just what he intended swimming in. Maybe it was time she got out. She heard a splash, felt the surge of water from his dive and turned to see him powering down the pool, long strokes eating up the length until he disappeared on a roll and came surging back towards her.

Maybe she should get out.

Maybe...

And then he was there beside her, water flying from his glorious head in beads that spun away like jewels in the silver of the moon.

'Couldn't sleep?' he asked her, and she shook her head, not wanting to open her mouth lest she reveal what had kept her awake.

Besides, his eyes had her full attention, night sky meeting the night sky, with just the glint of the moon to light them. They should be cold, she thought idly, but instead they were charged with heat and she wondered—*dared to hope*—that he might be fighting his own internal battle with temperature control.

He lifted a hand to her face, those dark eyes focused and intent, and her breath hitched as he pushed away a strand of wet hair from her face. His touch triggered sparks under her skin that travelled the entire length of her, a chain reaction that tugged at her nipples and sent a pulsing awareness between her thighs. 'I meant to thank you,' he said, 'for what you have done with the nursery. Rosa said you did it all yourself. Everything.'

Breathless, she struggled to find the words to answer. 'It was a job. It was good to have something to do.'

His eyes gleamed. 'You like to keep busy.'

'I like having something to do.'

'What will you do now it's finished?'

'I don't know. I haven't thought about it.'

'I have an idea,' he said, his hand curling around her neck, subtly but deliberately drawing her closer. 'If you were interested.'

'What does it involve?'

'It's not really a job as such,' he told her, his lips agonisingly close to her mouth. 'More a pastime.'

'What are the conditions?'

'Very favourable. Although,' he added, his lips brushing her cheek, tickling her eyelashes, kissing the tip of her nose as he drew her against him length to length, 'I have to warn you, there are some long night shifts involved.'

What was he offering her? That she become his mistress? That she warm his bed at night and grow his child by day? Should she be outraged? Her mind tried to make sense of it all but her brain was marshmallow under his slow sensual onslaught and right now, pressed up against his slick, tightly wound body, their legs tangling underwater and his hand weaving through her hair, outrage was the last thing she felt. Hadn't she secretly yearned for him to come after her? Hadn't she secretly prayed it was not just a one-night stand?

His teeth nipped an ear lobe and she gasped, feeling the tie at her neck release and his hand at her breast, rolling one slippery, hard nipple between his fingers. Oh, God, how was she supposed to think?

'Will I need a reference?' she asked, his mouth at her throat, the thick column of his erection nudging her belly, answering an earlier question in graphic, carnal detail.

'No reference required,' he gasped, his mouth over her nipple, his tongue working at the pebbled peak, driving her wild with need. 'Just an interview. Easy questions.'

He asked one of those questions now, tugging at her bikini bottoms. She answered by letting him push them down and curling her legs around him, opening himself for him.

His mouth was finally on hers, finally tearing her soul out again in a gut-wrenching kiss that left her almost shattered and ended only with the need to breathe. 'It sounds tempting,' she gasped, 'but how can I be sure I'm the right person you're looking for?'

He surged into her, hard and fast and deep and she took his glorious length to her heart, crying out with the effort. 'Believe me,' he told her through gritted teeth as he slowly withdrew, 'you're perfect.'

She came in a blaze of shooting stars—wave after endless wave of stars that splintered and shattered with his shuddering climax—and a solitary tear escaped from her eye.

You're perfect, he'd told her. *You're perfect.*

Nobody had ever said those words to her, nobody but her mother. But he'd said those words. He'd said them as if he believed them and he'd made her believe them. And her heart hoped and prayed. Surely he must love her, just a little?

He never told her she'd got the position, not officially, and he didn't move her things into his room, but she spent plenty of nights there in his arms—those nights he didn't come padding into her room in the dead of night.

His mood changed too. He was back to his old self. He'd visit the kitchen, spend time there with her and Rosa, sampling dishes and stealing breadsticks and even kisses when Rosa's back was turned and he got the chance.

And Angie felt herself fall deeper and deeper in love, dreading the day this child would be born. On the kitchen wall the calendar mocked her, every page turned bringing her closer to the inevitable—closer to the birth, closer to her departure until there was only one month to go.

Dominic said nothing about afterwards. He made love

to her tenderly at night and he took her out for dinner on Rosa's days off and walks along rugged coastal paths on perfect autumn days, and her heart ached and grew heavy like the baby inside her.

She loved him. She loved him as she had loved no other and she loved this child because it was part of him. It would break her heart to leave them both. But what choice did she have? She would not beg to stay on, especially after all the trouble he'd gone to to secure her house. She would not plead. She would walk out with her head, if not her heart, held high. She could not bear it if he rejected her.

It would kill her.

It was finished. Dominic held it up in his hands, in awe of the power of his grandfather's tools, in awe of the beauty they had created.

He didn't know if she'd like it or even want it, but it was done and he would give it to her as a gift when the baby was born. Something shifted in his chest and he looked at his watch. *So soon.*

He didn't want her to go. He wanted to tear up their agreement and keep her here. She belonged here, even if she'd never wanted this baby. And a question he'd wanted to put to her months ago—a possibility—surged back.

It had to be worth a try.

'Stay,' he said, as they lay together in the sweet afterglow of tender loving that night. 'Don't leave.'

Her heart bumped against a chest getting rapidly more crowded by the day, hope blossoming large but still too afraid to breathe.

'What do you mean?'

He raised himself on one elbow, looking down at her. 'There's no reason for you to go. Not really.'

But what reason is there for me to stay? She licked her lips. 'We have an agreement. I promised I wouldn't change my mind. I wouldn't cause any problems for you after the birth.'

'You wouldn't cause any problems! You'd be great. Rosa would love you to stay.'

And Dominic? What would Dominic love? Who did he love?

'And I know you never wanted this baby, but you'd be good with it, I know. You could help Rosa, don't you see, it would be perfect.'

Perfect.

'You want me to stay and help with the baby after it's born.'

He traced the fingers of one hand down the side of her face, his now familiar touch still causing her eyelashes to flutter and her breathing to hitch. 'I know how hard it would be for you, how much you were looking forward to being free, but it wouldn't be all bad, surely.'

His eyes shone with wicked intent, his hand now skimming her breast, but there was hope mixed in there too, she saw.

And he was so wrong. He was offering her some kind of miracle—the opportunity to hold this tiny infant, to feel its new baby breath on her cheek—he had no idea the world he was offering her!

But he wasn't asking her to stay because he loved her. She would have him in his bed but she would not have *him*. Women like her could not expect to have men like him.

'How long?' she ventured. 'How long would you expect me to stay?' *Before you throw me out.*

And immediately his hand stilled on her thigh. 'Would it be such a chore? Was I wrong to ask you? Would you rather leave and go back to that house?'

And she shook her head, for even without love, even without certainty or any degree of permanence, what he was offering her was one thousand times better than the alternative—returning to her little house, even if it was hers, alone with nothing but her thoughts and a shattered heart for company.

Who needed love when that was the alternate future you faced?

'I'll do it,' she said softly, 'I'll stay.'

She was in the kitchen making salad when she felt it—the sharp stabbing pain that stole her breath and doubled her over. She clutched at the bench, wincing as another pain sliced through her. 'What is it?' shrieked Rosa, running from the other end of the kitchen.

'I don't know,' she gasped, knowing only that it was a thousand times worse than the Braxton-Hicks contractions she was getting used to, fear curling down her spine. 'It's way too early.'

Rosa got her a chair, helped her to sit. 'Hold on, I'll call Dominic.'

Another shooting pain ripped through her, making her cry out with the intensity and with the sensation that something inside her was tearing free, the trickling flow that ran down her leg and spilled red against the tiled floor confirming it.

And panic flared inside her as another wrenching pain gripped her like a vice and Rosa's face at the phone turned white.

No! she thought in her last seconds before the pain took her away. *She could not lose this child! She wanted this child. She wanted her baby.*

CHAPTER ELEVEN

WHAT the hell was going on? Dominic paced back and forth in the waiting room, a cold sweat blanketing him, waiting for news he felt as if he'd already been waiting on for hours.

What the hell were they doing in there?

Rosa's panicked call—*'Angelina...the baby'*—had told him everything he'd needed to know. He'd swept out of the office like a cyclone, not knowing what was wrong, desperate to be there, learning along the way they'd taken her straight to Emergency.

And he still didn't understand what was happening, not beyond what Rosa had told him. She'd collapsed in the kitchen and there'd been blood. A haemorrhage, the paramedics had apparently radioed ahead. A haemorrhage could not be good. A haemorrhage sounded bad.

He stopped pacing, clawed his fingers through his hair and saw Rosa huddled on a chair with her eyes closed in an ashen face, her fingers interwoven, her lips moving silently.

Praying for Angelina.

Praying for the unborn baby.

And a tsunami of terror washed over him, drenching

him in a fear like no other. Rosa had been there. Rosa
had seen it happen. Rosa had seen the blood.

Surely it wouldn't come to that?

Surely he couldn't lose them?

Not now.

He sat alongside Rosa, her face now still, and pulled
her against him. She went willingly, as if she needed his
support, and he wished he'd thought to hold her earlier,
to share her pain. But how could you think when something like this happened? How could you survive?

A woman appeared, still wearing scrubs, fresh from
Theatre, and they both jumped to their feet, still hold-
ing on. 'Mr Pirelli? You have a beautiful baby daughter.
She's going to be fine. We'll let you see her soon.'

He closed his eyes. Uttered up his own small prayer
of thanks. It was something. Some measure of relief.
Good news. But it wasn't anywhere near enough.

'And Angelina? What about Angelina?'

'The surgeons are still with her. She's had a rough
time.' She gave an apologetic smile. 'We'll let you know
the moment we know anything more.'

He sat back down, Rosa following, still clinging to
his hand. 'A baby girl,' she sniffed with tear-filled eyes.
'That's wonderful,' before her tears became a torrent and
he pulled her against him.

'She'll be all right,' he said. 'Angelina will be all
right. She's a fighter. She's strong. Nothing can happen
to her.' And he willed himself to believe it, to be strong
himself, to not think about losing the woman he loved.

He raised his eyes to the ceiling. Oh, my God. She
was the light at the end of a long day. She was his every
night time fantasy. She was the woman who had found
him and grounded him and brought him back to life.
She was the woman who had risked her very life to bear

his child. Why had it taken something like this to make him see?

Of course he loved her.

And he could not lose her now.

The minutes ticked away—minutes where regret loomed large. She would come home, he told himself, and he would take care of her. He would love her and cherish her. And maybe, one day, she might love him and the baby too. Maybe.

But he would do whatever he could to make it happen.

A door opened. The nurse appeared again, this time pushing a nursery trolley. 'Here is your baby, Mr Pirelli, if you'd like to say hello and get acquainted.'

He looked down at the tiny infant, red-faced and squirming, with a shock of black hair and a mouth testing the air.

'Would you like to hold your daughter?'

He wasn't sure. She was so tiny, so very fragile. And right now, with the tangle of emotions inside him, he wasn't even sure he wanted to. Angelina was still in Theatre, fighting for her life because of this tiny scrap. But before he could place his big hands under her tiny body and lift her to his chest, a doctor arrived, his brow sheened with sweat, his mask pulled below his chin and a smile on his lips.

'Mrs Cameron is going to be all right. She's in Recovery now.'

His head sagged in relief, tension drained from his bones, and the baby chose that moment to open her eyes and look up at him, frowning, as night sky met night sky.

Mine, he thought with a surge of pride. *The baby and Angelina. Both mine.*

* * *

The next morning he stood at the door to her room. They hadn't let him visit last night, no more than a glance he'd got on his way out and then she'd been hooked up to so many machines he wasn't sure he could have stayed. This morning there were fewer machines and he could cope. Besides, he had something important to tell her.

Her eyes were closed and at first he thought she was asleep, but as he neared the bed her eyelids fluttered open.

'Dominic.' Her voice was hoarse and weak, but his name on her lips was suddenly one of his favourite sounds. 'I'm so sorry.'

'Why should you be sorry?' he asked, putting the parcel down before pressing his lips to her brow, scared to bump her and cause her more pain.

'I thought I was going to lose the baby. I thought I was going to lose…' She didn't finish on a hiccup, just squeezed her eyes shut.

'Shh,' he said, taking her hand gently in his, careful not to knock the cannula anchoring her drip. 'The baby's fine. Have you seen her?'

She shook her head against the pillow. 'Not yet.' He wondered if it was because she wasn't interested or because she couldn't bear to. He wouldn't blame her. But he'd told them last night she wouldn't be feeding the child. He wouldn't subject her to that when she'd never wanted this child, so maybe the nurses were looking after her.

'I'm sorry for what you had to go through to have her,' he admitted. 'If I'd had any idea, I would never have let you take that risk.'

She shrugged. 'It was a fluke, the doctors said. One in a million chance. Sheer dumb luck it happened to me.'

But it had happened to her. And it had made him realise...

'So have you decided on a name?'

'I have. And Rosa agrees with me. I decided she should have her mothers' names.'

Angie nodded tightly. For the last six months she'd lived under the shadow of that name, but it was the right thing to do. 'It's a pretty name.'

'I thought so. And it suits her. Angela Carla Pirelli. I was hoping you'd like it.'

She looked up at him, aghast. 'Angela? But you said—'

He kissed her fingertips. 'I said her mothers' names. *Plural*. You and Carla.'

Tears sprang to her eyes. 'But I have no right—'

And he smiled, or it looked almost like a smile—a smile that tugged at the fragile shreds of her heart that remained intact. 'You have more right than anyone to claim this child for your own. What a laboratory created with part of Carla and me was a mere possibility, nothing more than the chance of a child. But it was you who turned that dream into a reality, you who turned that chance into a flesh and blood baby. You made this child's life possible.'

'But—'

'Don't you understand? She is your child, Angelina, your baby. You have more rights to this child than anyone. You are her mother.'

Angie pressed her lips together, trying to quell the tears, though there was no way she could stem them all.

'You're crying,' he said. 'Did I say something wrong?'

'No. You said everything right.' She sniffed. 'In that case, do you think I could see my baby?'

And he smiled and pressed the call button. 'I'd like that.'

Within moments she arrived, swaddled in a fresh pink blanket. From where she lay, Angie could just see the black hair and one tiny hand sticking out under the chin. 'I've brought you a bottle too, Mr Pirelli,' the midwife said, 'in case you'd like to feed her.'

From the bed came a small mewling cry. They looked around.

'Do you think…?' Angelina asked. 'Is it possible… Is there any chance I might be able to feed her?'

'Are you sure?' he asked.

'Are you up to it?' the midwife asked, and Angie sniffed and nodded.

'I'd really like to try.'

Minutes later they had her raised and pillowed for protection. It seemed a mammoth effort for such a tiny creature but, when the midwife placed her on her pillowed lap, it was all worth it. She looked down at this infant, this baby she'd harboured inside her body for nearly nine months, this miracle child, and fell instantly and irrevocably in love. 'Hello, Angela Carla Pirelli,' she said as a tiny hand wrapped around her finger and her heartstrings at the same time. 'You're one very lucky little girl. You've got two mothers—the one who made you so very beautiful, and me.'

The midwife sniffled and swiped at her eyes, becoming brusque and businesslike. 'Let's get you organised then, shall we?' She showed Angie how to get the baby to latch on. Angie was a quick learner. The baby was even quicker and soon she was contentedly suckling.

Beautiful, Dominic thought as he watched mother and child together. Truly beautiful.

'This is the woman,' he whispered in awed reverence

when the midwife had departed and the baby had fallen asleep, 'who never wanted a child. Look at you. You're a natural. What happened?'

She shrugged, and smiled down at the baby in her arms, lifted her and drank in her magical new baby scent. 'I didn't want a baby. At least, not with Shayne. I know that now. I was happy when I found out it wasn't his. And then I was afraid to get attached to this little one because I knew I would be leaving. I couldn't afford to love it, even though, as it grew and as I felt it move inside, I couldn't help but feel a connection.' She sighed, a slow sad smile emerging. 'I tried to fight it. I tried to keep my distance because I knew I'd end up hurt. But it was impossible.'

'Marry me.'

She blinked and looked up at his brusque demand. 'What did you say?'

'Marry me, Angelina. Become my wife.'

She shook her head. She was dreaming, the painkillers affecting her brain. 'Don't think you have to marry me. You don't have to try to make up for what happened. It was an accident.'

'I don't want to marry you because I feel guilty for what happened.'

A frisson of fear zipped down her spine. 'But you can't marry me. Look at where I come from. What would people think?'

'I don't care what people think. You know that.'

'But people will still talk.'

'And all they will discover is that we grew up three blocks and however many years apart. Yes, Angelina,' he said in answer to her look of disbelief, 'I spent the first fifteen years of my life in the very next suburb. I lived there with my nonna and poppa, and mother, until none of them were left, then I was determined to find their house by the sea for them. The home they never had.'

He smiled. 'So you see, there's no reason why you should refuse me now, surely.'

'But I still don't understand why you want to.'

He took one of her hands in his and gave her a crooked grin. 'Why? Because I love you. I was too damned stupid to admit it or even recognise it before, but nearly losing you made me realise that I love you.'

Even under the sensation-numbing drugs being pumped into her body, she could still feel the unmistakable trip of her heart, and the swell of emotion as hope sprouted and blossomed into something magnificent. Something real. *Real.* There was that word again—the word that seemed to surround this man from the moment she'd met him.

Yet still she dared not believe it could be true. 'But Carla. I thought you were still in love with Carla. This is her child. I thought that's why you wanted it so much.'

He smiled a sad smile, reaching over to brush his baby's hair, skimming his thumb over her brow. 'Carla will always have a place in my heart.'

'She was so very beautiful.'

He nodded. 'She was, and yet so brittle at the same time.' He turned his eyes from his sleeping child to the woman holding her. 'She wasn't like you, Angelina, so strong and resilient. Carla always wanted what she couldn't have, thinking it would make her happy, thinking it would be enough. But nothing was ever enough for her. Money wasn't enough. The house wasn't enough. Still she wasn't happy.

'And then she decided a baby would make her happy. But by then she was already losing weight, already starving herself. There was no way she could conceive and no way she would listen to anyone.'

He sighed. 'When I first met you, you reminded me of how she looked. So gaunt and half-starved. I couldn't understand why you had been able to grow this child, when she hadn't.'

'You said you hated me back then.'

'I know.' He blew out through his teeth. 'I didn't know you. I didn't trust you. I was angry.'

His hand dropped to hers again. 'I was so wrong. It was like I'd built a stone wall around my heart. I hadn't been able to save Carla with all the money in the world. All it took was one simple infection. Anyone else would have had the strength to fight it off. She had nothing to fight with.'

Angie looked down at the baby in her arms, her heart squeezed tight.

'I didn't want to have to save anyone else,' he continued. 'When you turned up on the scene with my baby in your belly, it was like you had started shaking those walls at their very foundations. And I didn't want them coming down. I fought it every step of the way.

'You brought them down, and you grounded me and brought me back to life, just as you have given life to our child. So believe me when I tell you, I want to be with you for ever. I want you to be my wife. I love you, Angelina, and one day I hope you can find a way to love me too, after all that I have put you through.'

She looked up at him, blinking through misty eyes.

'I do love you, Dominic. It's been so hard these past few months, loving you.' And the tears came then—tears of joy. Tears of relief. Tears of love.

He sat next to her on the bed and cradled her head in

his arm, one hand behind his baby's head. 'Then you'll marry me.'

She sniffed and nodded and cried some more and now she looked a complete and utter mess and still she could not stop herself, she was so deliriously happy. And as if he sensed her fears, he kissed her eyes, kissed away her tears. He took the sleeping infant from her arms and placed her back in her crib and reached down for the package he'd brought with him.

'I didn't think to get a ring,' he said apologetically. 'But I'd like you to have this.' He handed her the parcel, wrapped in simple gold tissue paper, tied with a red ribbon.

She looked at it and then up to him, the question in her eyes. 'Open it,' he prompted, suddenly nervous.

Paper crinkled and tore even though she took care as she unrolled the gift. And then she gasped, lifting the carving free from the wrapping in her hands, turning it one way and then the other. The woman stood, one leg bent, her head angled down, her face looking down as her hands cradled the baby within her belly. She was long-limbed and slim with hair that floated in layers down to her naked breasts. 'It's beautiful,' she said, awed by the work of art, awed even more by the mystery surrounding it. 'But it's me! Wherever did you find it?'

'Do you remember, a long time ago, you once told me I didn't actually make anything?'

'No, Dominic!' One hand went to her mouth. 'I was wrong—so wrong. I was looking for reasons not to like you. I was clutching at straws.'

He pulled her hand away, shaking his head. 'You were right. I was so busy making money, I'd forgotten how to actually make things. Real things. My poppa once taught me to carve. You inspired me to pick up those tools—'

'Hardly inspired!'

He gave a wry smile. 'Okay, so you goaded me into picking up his tools. And it was harder than I remembered—much harder, and nothing worked. But one night I saw you coming out of the pool and standing there, wringing out your hair, your belly ripening with my child, and I knew I had to capture you. You brought me home, Angelina. You made me realise what was real again.'

Moisture made her lashes thick and heavy. 'It's beautiful, Dominic, just beautiful.'

'You're beautiful, Angelina. You will always be beautiful to me. Do you like it?'

'Like it? I love it.' And she looked up at him. 'Nearly as much as I love you.'

And he dipped his head to kiss her. 'Hold that thought.'

EPILOGUE

ANGELA CARLA PIRELLI, or AC-DC as she'd become
fondly known, a reference to both her first two initials
and to her high octane energy levels, attended her first
wedding aged six and a half months.

According to her, this party was all about her, and
given the way she was passed from guest to guest, made
to chuckle endlessly with tickles and funny faces and
peekaboo, and generally clucked, oohed and aahed over,
it was no wonder she assumed she was the star of the
show.

Dominic knew differently.

He loved his tiny daughter immensely. Would gladly
give his life for her.

But in his eyes, there was only one star on this day of
days and his eyes drank in the vision of her as she approached, everyone in between wanting to congratulate
her after their wedding in the gazebo, everyone wanting
to compliment her on the way she looked. He could understand why. In that Grecian-inspired gown falling in
folds around her perfect body and with her hair pinned
up in sections leaving coiling trails around her face and
throat, she looked like a goddess. Already he could feel
another stint in the garage coming on.

Mind you, the next one would take a while. He didn't

intend spending too much time down there at night in the foreseeable future.

Dominic was momentarily distracted as he heard his daughter's chuckling laugh ringing out in delight. Rosa had her on her hip, he saw, bouncing her up and down in time to the music.

'I do believe that daughter of yours is going to be a handful in a few years' time.'

He turned to her as his new wife slipped a slender arm through his and he almost wanted to growl with pleasure that she was his. 'So now she's my daughter,' he said, raising a questioning brow. 'I thought we were equals in this role.'

'Most of the time,' she said as he handed her a glass of champagne from a passing tray.

'Oh, and what's that supposed to mean?'

And Angie just smiled as Rosa passed the child to the man alongside her, who clearly hadn't expected an infant to land in his arms. For a second he looked shocked, as if he didn't know what to do with her, but then she batted her dark eyes at him and smiled a baby-toothed smile and he warmed to her, suddenly laughing and jigging her up and down, her squeals of delight ringing out.

'There you go,' she said, 'exactly my point. Unexpected woman meets unwelcoming man, falls in love with him and wins his heart. That is definitely my daughter out there.'

He smiled, pulling her close to him. 'What do you think a son of ours would be like?'

'Dangerous,' she said without thinking. 'A heart stopper. Likes fast cars and sleek women and knows how to use them both.'

'Ouch, I think.'

'Oh, no,' she said. 'It's not all bad. Because he's a

keeper, this son of ours. And some lucky girl will get to keep him for ever.'

He pulled her into his embrace, wanting more than anything for her to open the tiny half-joking wedding gift he'd left under her pillow, the lace-edged pinny he was hanging out for her to wear so they could go to work on that upcoming son, forgetting for a moment his child and the crowd and the music and lights all around them. 'Will you keep me for ever, Mrs Pirelli?'

And she gazed up into his dark-as-night eyes. 'Only if they won't let me keep you longer. I love you, Dominic, for ever.'

And as he kissed his brand-new wife, the mother of his child, he knew forever would never be long enough.

One night with a hot-blooded male!

18th February 2011

18th March 2011

15th April 2011

20th May 2011

2 FREE BOOKS
AND A SURPRISE GIFT

We would like to take this opportunity to thank you for reading this Mills & Boon® book by offering you the chance to take TWO more specially selected books from the Modern™ series absolutely FREE! We're also making this offer to introduce you to the benefits of the Mills & Boon® Book Club™—

- **FREE home delivery**
- **FREE gifts and competitions**
- **FREE monthly Newsletter**
- **Exclusive Mills & Boon Book Club offers**
- **Books available before they're in the shops**

Accepting these FREE books and gift places you under no obligation to buy, you may cancel at any time, even after receiving your free books. Simply complete your details below and return the entire page to the address below. You don't even need a stamp!

YES Please send me 2 free Modern books and a surprise gift. I understand that unless you hear from me, I will receive 4 superb new books every month for just £3.30 each, postage and packing free. I am under no obligation to purchase any books and may cancel my subscription at any time. The free books and gift will be mine to keep in any case.

Ms/Mrs/Miss/Mr _____ Initials _____

Surname _____

Address _____

_____

_____ Postcode _____

E-mail _____

Send this whole page to: Mills & Boon Book Club, Free Book Offer, FREEPOST NAT 10298, Richmond, TW9 1BR